Henrietta's Home

Book 10 in Clover Creek Caravan
Kirsten Osbourne

Chapter One

Tuesday, October 19th, 1852

I cannot believe we're almost back to Clover Creek. We've been walking since March, and I'm exhausted, but soon we will be in our new home, and we will be able to build our houses and businesses and start living and not just trying to reach a destination so we can begin our lives.

The journey has been long and hard. My mother passed on the way between Oregon City and Clover Creek, and I've taken over the cooking from her. Thankfully, all my brothers are older than I am, and I do not have to worry about taking care of them like some of the other young ladies who lost their mothers.

The excitement filling the camp today is filling me with delight for the first time since my mother died along the way. My father is still fulfilling his duties as captain, but soon it will no longer be necessary. Eventually our little community may need a mayor, but that will be down the road.

Pa is planning to start a ranch there near the creek where he chose his plot of land. I know he is having difficulties with losing Ma, but I have a feeling he will be able to do all he needs to do anyway. Pa is one of those people who just keeps going and going.

We should reach Clover Creek before noon today, and we will all find our exact plots of land, and then we will start building a community.

*I do wish we'd had a bit more time for me to get up the courage
to talk to Roy Williams. I have had my eye on him since we first
started on the trail. He never once asked me to dance, though I
do wish he had.*

Henrietta Appleby, the youngest of Jacob Appleby's children, stretched
to get the kinks out from sleeping on the ground for so long, and
then she walked to the fire to start breakfast for her father and three
older brothers. Each of her brothers had gotten their own plot of land,
but she would be living with her father. At eighteen, she'd been too
young to get her own plot of land without being married. If she'd been
married, she and her husband could have each gotten one. But you had
to be twenty-one to stake a claim if you were unmarried.

Henrietta didn't mind, but she did think her own land would make
her more appealing to potential suitors. Of which she hoped Roy
would be at the head of the line. Never in her life had she so badly
wanted to go up to a man and ask him to court her, but she knew it
would be unacceptable behavior. Her mother had always told her she
needed to chase a man until he caught her, which seemed like good
advice, but it was considered forward to chase a man, and she didn't
think seeming forward would be a good idea.

Roy was on the trail with his own parents and three younger sisters,
and she knew he'd staked his own claim. So, he was over twenty-one,
and not married yet. If there was just a way, she could get him to talk
to her. But all day, he drove his own wagon. Some of the essentials that
his parents needed were in the back of his wagon as well, and he was an
integral part of the Williams family making it to Clover Creek.

After making johnny cakes for breakfast, she woke her father and
brothers, who all preferred to get the last minute of sleep they could
and then rush through their chores before they pulled out of camp for
the day.

Her brothers had each brought their own wagon, but they tended to park theirs right beside their father's so they could eat the meals her mother had cooked, and now the meals she cooked.

When they'd all relieved themselves, they joined her at the small fire she'd made for their meal. They'd loaded up on as many supplies as possible as they'd gone through Soda Springs again, and most of them felt they were going to be ready for winter if they had roofs over their heads.

Henri, as her family called her, knew her father planned on a simple cabin for the first winter, but if he had time, he would build a real house during the warmer months. Her brothers all had the same plans, and she thought it would be good if they found wives, but not one of them seemed to think they should until they were established in Clover Creek.

She had to wonder if Roy felt the same. His sisters were close to her age, but she'd never sought them out to walk beside them. Usually she'd walked alongside her mother, and they'd chatted along the way. She knew the Williams sisters were the same. They stuck together and walked with their mother as they moved along.

Her brothers were all eating when Henri decided she would walk with Roy's family that day. She'd taken to walking with Jane and Sarah most days, helping them look over the children as she did, but she was going to do something new that day. If she could make friends with his sisters, perhaps they could see one another even after they'd settled.

"I think you should save the breakfast dishes for tonight when we're camped on our own property. The creek will provide all the water you need for your chores," Pa said.

Henri nodded. "I can do that. It sounds a great deal more pleasant than trying to do them before we leave this morning. I haven't gotten water from the river yet this morning."

"I told your brothers they should be carrying your water for you." Pa looked between Jared, Samuel, and Sebastian. "Have you not been doing as you were told?"

Jared shrugged. "I thought Sam and Bastian were doing it."

Sam sighed. "I thought Jared and Bastian were doing it."

Pa looked at Bastian. "I guess you thought your brothers were doing it as well?"

Bastian nodded, grinning. Bastian was always in a jovial mood. He had been Henri's favorite brother since she was tiny. He was the youngest of her brothers, so it made sense she was closest to him.

"I manage, Pa." She didn't want to make a big deal out of the work she did for her family. It was women's work after all.

"Yes, you manage, but you are cooking for the three of them, and they need to show you some respect. You could start refusing to cook for any of them, and just cook for the two of us. Then where would they be?"

"Hungry," Henrietta said with a grin.

"I'm serious about this. If your brothers don't bring you water and firewood once we get to Clover Creek, then you will stop cooking for them. They need to be thankful for all you do for them as the only woman in the family left." Pa shook his head. "I feel like they are taking advantage of your kindness."

"Yes, Pa." Henri knew she'd sneak food to her brothers if it came to that. They could be a pain in her backside, but she loved them all.

"We should be in Clover Creek by noon. I want to go to our property and start building that log cabin. You boys will help me build one with a loft for Henri and me, and then I'll help you with yours. It would be smart if you three could share a cabin this winter and then build your own when it warms up, but that's up to you, and I'll help with whatever you decide to build."

"I don't want to have to worry about sharing a house with my brothers when I start courting. We had a lot of pretty girls for traveling companions." Jared, the eldest, said.

Henri was startled to realize her brothers were thinking of starting to court girls before winter, but in a way, it made sense to her. She had no desire to settle into a cabin with her pa and then have to move everything later. After walking two-thousand miles, she felt like she wanted to be done moving for a while.

"Do you already have your eye on someone?" Henri asked, not expecting a real answer.

"Emma Williams. She's the prettiest girl available, so I need to move in quickly to get her to realize I'm the person she wants to marry."

Henri frowned. Did all men want to marry the prettiest girl? With her brown hair and dark eyes, she knew she wasn't the prettiest girl around, but she hoped her delicate features made up for her coloring.

Henri looked between Samuel and Bastian. "Do you two have girls in mind?"

Both brothers shook their heads. "I'm waiting til spring," Bastian said. "That's when all the animals find mates. I'll follow their lead."

Henrietta laughed. Bastian was ridiculous.

Sam shrugged. "I'll wait, but not necessarily try to find someone in spring. When the right girl comes along, I'll know it."

"And are you both looking for the prettiest girls?"

Bastian looked thoughtful for a moment. "Some things are more important than how a girl looks. Like cooking. You cook like a dream! I'd marry you if you weren't my sister."

Henri shook her head, laughing. "So, all that matters is a girl who can cook? It doesn't matter if she's not pretty?"

"Not as much as whether she can cook. I'd rather not have to put a bag over her head to make babies, of course, but I will if I need to!"

"Bastian! We do not talk about things like that with women," Pa glowered at Bastian.

Sam half-grinned. "I agree with Bastian that there's more to marriage than how pretty a girl is. I want someone I can have real conversations with. Someone that doesn't mind helping with the chores and will be a good mother. Sometimes pretty girls are the worst candidates for a wife because they think everything is beneath them."

As she listened to her brothers discuss what they wanted in a wife, Henri's insecurities grew by leaps and bounds. Was she the kind of woman any man would want to marry? "So, what happens to the girls who aren't really pretty, and who don't cook well or care to take on ranch chores?"

Bastian looked at her for a moment before throwing his head back and laughing. "You're worried you won't get married! That's hilarious. You're prettier than Emma Williams by far. We all just have to keep overlooking you because you're our sister. Trust me, it won't be long before Pa has a line at his door filled with men who want to court you."

Henri stood up and tucked the dishes back into the back of the wagon. Bastian's compliment was nice, but it wasn't enough. She needed to hear something like that from a male who wasn't her brother.

Bastian followed her to the wagon and asked in a whisper, "Who do you have your eye on?"

Henri blushed, looking at him. "Why do you think I have my eye on someone?"

"Because you've never cared about being pretty or the best at chores and cooking. I can see right on your face there's a boy you're sweet on."

Henri bit her lip as she thought about telling her brother who it was, and finally, after some contemplation, she whispered, "Roy Williams." She hoped he wouldn't laugh at her. She truly wanted his approval.

Bastian nodded. "He's a good man. I like the idea of you marrying him."

"Don't tell anyone." She would hate it if it got all over camp that she was setting her cap for Roy.

"I wouldn't. Though, I may try to play matchmaker for the two of you. I need a way to entertain myself." With that, Bastian headed off to get the oxen he needed for his wagon. They'd brought more oxen than anyone else around, but they planned to build a huge ranch, with all four of the men working together.

Henri wanted to run after her brother and tell him in no uncertain terms that she didn't want him to interfere, but she didn't want to be seen running which would look unladylike. But more than that, she knew if she told her brother to keep his nose out of her business, he would be all the more determined.

She decided not to make the effort to walk with Roy's sisters and mother that day. It would seem like she had instigated her brother talking to Roy if she did. And while she had told him who she had set her cap for, she hadn't wanted him to talk to him. Not at all.

Soon, they were back on the trail for their last day. Their beautiful home would be able to be seen over the next mountain. They all walked up, and then she saw it. The beautiful valley that almost the entire company had decided to settle in. Clover Creek, where every day would be wonderful. Henri couldn't wait to sleep on her father's land that night.

It was just before noon that the entire party stopped near the creek. Pa walked out into the middle of the wagons, where he could be heard by everyone. "We've all put in a great deal of work to get here, to our new home. I want to thank all of you for coming along this journey with us. I know we've lost more than our share of people along the way, and we will always miss those who have gone before us as a result of this journey. We will always mourn with you." He turned to the pastor who was standing close. "Pastor Scott? Would you thank God for his mercies in bringing us to our destination?"

Jed stepped forward and bowed his head, praying for the people they'd lost along the way, and asking for them to be forever in their hearts. And he prayed the community would be blessed with good people and bountiful crops and livestock. When he'd finished, there was a loud resounding "amen" that carried throughout the valley.

Pa said, "As your captain, I thank you once again for the journey, and I pray we all have wonderful lives starting from this day forward. My family and I claimed the land at the top of that hill." He pointed to a large hill, which was very close. "If you need help, come see us, and we'll be happy to oblige. I hope the rest of you feel the same. We've journeyed so far together, that it would be terrible to lose the friendships we've forged along the way."

George Bedwell stepped forward. "You're going to need help making it up that hill there. Would you allow us to be part of your homecoming?"

Pa looked at the former captain before nodding. "We would appreciate any help you'd be willing to give us."

Henri couldn't believe Mr. Bedwell had been the one to offer to help them get their things up the hill. He'd not been the most pleasant man in the beginning, but his wife Katie had taught him a great deal about love and being kind to others.

Many of the men gathered to unload some of the belongings from the back of each of the wagons, so that they wouldn't be too heavy to make it up the hill. And then they started their slow ascent.

Henri was surprised when Roy fell into step beside her. "Are you excited to have the most coveted property in the whole settlement?" he asked.

"Why is it the most coveted?"

"Because of the view. I think your pa should put your house right there on that little plateau. That way you can watch the town grow as you do your dishes."

She smiled. "That does sound wonderful."

"Would you say you'd be welcome to having a suitor come to see you whenever he had the chance?" Roy asked, surprising her.

Henri felt her throat constrict. What had Bastian said to him? She nodded, not sure how to speak any longer. This was a day she'd been hoping for since March.

"Good. I'll talk to your pa about it. I've had my eye on you since Independence."

"You have?" It made no sense. Why hadn't he asked her to dance? Or to walk with him?

"Of course," he said, smiling down at her.

"Why haven't you approached me before now, then?" she asked, wondering the whole time if she was being too pushy by asking.

"Because we weren't at our destination. I couldn't have lived through losing you on that horrible journey."

She looked over at him to see if he looked serious. "Really?"

"Really!"

"Then please, talk to my father. I would feel privileged to be courted by you. I know one of my brothers wants to court your sister Emma now that we're here."

"Perhaps our children will have double cousins." He reached down to grasp her hand. "Do you mind?"

"Not even a little."

They were breathing heavily by the time they'd reached the top of the steep hill, but nothing was lost. As her father and brothers headed down the hill for the things they'd taken out so they could make it up the hill, she started gathering wood for their fire.

Roy was beside her the entire time, and when they'd brought enough firewood and kindling for a few days, he said, "I'll get you a bucket of water as well. Then I'll be off to start my ranch."

"Where is your land?" she asked.

"Just at the base of this hill," he told her.

Henri smiled. "Then it won't be too hard for you to come and talk to my father later. I know he didn't see us holding hands, but I also know he's heard by now. He won't be happy if you don't talk to him and make it official that we're courting."

"Happy to do that, and no, it won't be difficult at all. If all goes well, I'd like to be married by winter."

She glanced at him and blushed. "I think that sounds lovely."

Chapter Two

Tuesday, October 19th, 1852

Today has been a truly glorious day. We made it to Clover Creek, and I was approached by the brother of the girl I've had my eye on since Independence, Missouri. He told me that he thought his sister and I would make a great couple. I'd already planned to approach Henrietta as soon as we got to Clover Creek, but I would have probably waited another day or two.

I'll go see her pa in the morning after my chores, and I'll ask if I may court her. For now, I'm living on the land my father was granted, but I will be building a one room cabin quickly. I'm glad our families ended up settling so close together, and I hope her father accepts me as a prospective suitor for her.

I will probably stop my journal entries after this one. There is no need to continue since this was my trail diary, and we're no longer moving along the trail, though we are living on it.

It will seem odd not to write a journal entry every day, and I must admit, I enjoyed doing it once I'd started. I hope my days will now be spent building my cabin, taking care of livestock, and courting my lovely Henrietta. It is very clear she likes the idea as much as I do.

On Wednesday morning, Roy did his morning chores, including milking the cows and gathering eggs. He thought gathering eggs was women's work, so he wasn't sure why he was expected to do it instead of his sisters. But Pa said it was his job, and he wasn't about to disobey his father. He didn't care how old he was.

He took the milk to the spot where his mother and sisters had dubbed their kitchen, which he found downright silly. Their kitchen consisted of a barrel of rainwater and a campfire. He and his father would build a bench and a table soon, and then they had to get started on the cabin. There was frost on the ground as he woke that morning, and he knew it wouldn't be long before they had snow. Perhaps this wasn't the best spot to move to in autumn. Either way, it was their land, and they would make the most of it.

After breakfast, he told his pa he needed to run up the hill for a moment, but he wouldn't be gone long. He couldn't be. There were trees to fell and use for making the cabin, and they had two cabins to make in a relatively short time.

"You'd better hurry back. We're digging a cellar today, and it's not going to be easy work."

Roy nodded. "I won't be long at all, and we'll get that cellar dug. Do I need a cellar for my cabin, or will Ma give me a little space for storing my own food?"

"Of course, your ma will give you space. Hurry!"

After his second instruction to hurry, Roy hurried up the hill as fast as he could. Even after all those months of driving, climbing a hill that steep was difficult.

Once he reached the top, he slowed a bit until he caught his breath, and then he ran over to the spot where Henrietta had built a fire the day before. The family was still eating when he arrived, but he knew he couldn't wait for them to finish before talking to her pa. He had to get back.

"May I speak with you for a moment, Captain."

Mr. Appleby gave him a strange look. "We're not on the trail anymore, boy. It's Mr. Appleby now."

"May I speak with you?"

Mr. Appleby shrugged. "Have at it."

"Alone, please?" Roy didn't want to have this conversation with her brothers watching, and he certainly didn't want to have it in front of Henrietta.

Mr. Appleby sighed. "This had better be important. You're taking me from one of my daughter's meals, and she's even more skilled at cooking than her mother was." He got to his feet and walked away from the campfire a bit. "What is it?"

Roy took a deep breath, trying to ignore Mr. Appleby's gruff attitude. "I want to ask your permission to court Henrietta."

"Henri? I thought you declared you were courting her when you held her hand as we were climbing this hill yesterday."

Roy sighed. "She told me you'd know, and I needed to ask you as soon as possible."

"Henri was right. You should have asked me to court her before you ever touched her." Mr. Appleby looked him up and down. "My boys have said good things about you, so I'll say yes. You may court her."

"Thank you, sir. May I come by this evening after my pa and I have finished the work we have planned for the day?"

"You may. I want the two of you to be always within my sight or the sight of one of her brothers. You hear me?"

"Yes, sir. I will do that with no problem. Now, I must get back down the hill. My pa and I are digging a cellar today."

"Are you building your own cabin?" Mr. Appleby asked.

"As soon as we finish the one for my family," Roy said.

"Good. My girl does not need to be courted for a long time. Just get it done."

"I will." With that, Roy hurried down the hill to his father, who had only shoveled one clump of dirt. He had squared off the area to dig with some sticks and some thread.

Roy grabbed his own shovel and started digging.

"You courting that Appleby girl?" Pa asked.

Roy nodded. "I am. I had to ask her father for permission."

"You shoulda done that before you held her hand yesterday."

"I know. I knew it at the time, but I planned to ask to court her the first chance I got."

"Her pa said you could court her?"

"He did. I'm thankful. I've had my eye on her for a while."

"Shoulda asked her on the trail when we had weekly dances. Then you coulda walked at night and danced with her. Weren't thinking ahead, were you?"

"I guess not. I just wanted to be here, so we could court and marry quick."

"Do you think the captain will let you marry her quick?"

"He told me not to draw things out, so I guess he will." Roy had dug twice as much as his father at that point, and no longer felt guilty for leaving.

They worked steadily through the day and had a five and a half foot cellar built by the time they were ready to finish for the day. "Are you sure this is deep enough, Pa?"

"It'll only be your ma and sisters coming down here, and none of them is over five foot four. It's going to be just fine."

"So tomorrow the floors, and then we start walling it in on Friday?"

Pa nodded. "And we must remember that instead of working here on Sunday, we're all building the church. It'll be a log church, but there will be a building to worship in come winter."

"How long do you think the cabin will take us?"

"Probably a couple of weeks if we work hard and work fast, which we'll do. And then we'll work on yours. There will be no digging into partially frozen ground for yours and it'll be done quickly. If you stay with us while we work on it, it won't be so bad to wait that long."

"All right. I think we just need to do it then." He was already imagining bringing his beautiful bride home to the cabin they'd build. Every log would be placed with love.

"I know we do! And your sisters are on milking and eggs. I need you working every minute you can with me." Pa stretched, his back aching from the work they'd put in. "Your ma should have supper ready. This is the only night that will mean the end of our workday. Go visit your gal tonight but let her know tomorrow you'll be working from sun-up to sun-down. You can see her after it's dark if that's what you want to do."

At that moment, he wanted to collapse, but he would go see Henrietta—or Henri as her family called her. He'd said he would, and he wouldn't go back on his promise. Besides, he couldn't wait to see her and hold her hand again.

"I'll let her know. Maybe she and I can take a lunch together or something."

"You decide." Pa led the way to the campfire where the girls were all working on their meal.

"It's just about ready," Ma said. "It's just a stew, but I think it will be hearty enough to warm you up and give you the strength to work more tomorrow."

"That's all we need," Roy said, collapsing onto the ground. He and his pa needed to make them a table yet. But it probably wouldn't happen until after the cabin was built. And hopefully not until after *his* cabin was built as well. They could make furniture all winter.

As soon as they finished supper, Roy stood and hurried up the hill to the campfire there. The Appleby family had just finished eating.

"May I take your daughter for a walk, Mr. Appleby?"

"Yes, but stay within sight of us. If you can't see us, then you've gone too far."

"Yes, sir."

Henrietta stood, and they walked together, making a huge circle around her family's campfire. "I hate that my family feels the need to watch every step we take," she said in a whisper.

"I'm sure I'll do the same for our daughters," he said. "I know it sounds like I'm jumping the gun, but I really am courting you with an intent to marry."

She smiled at him. "That would make me happy as well."

"Good. Then I know why I'm working so hard." He squeezed her hand. For a moment he wished that her whole family wasn't watching them, and he could kiss her, but he was pretty sure it would be a problem. "I must start working sun-up to sun-down tomorrow. Pa and I dug an entire cellar today. Tomorrow we'll be chopping down trees for their floor and building a hatch over stairs to get to the cellar. And then we'll start the outer walls. With both of us working together, we should be able to get it done in a couple of weeks, and then we'll start on my cabin. I won't have a cellar, but Ma will let me store food in hers." He was giving her this information because she would be the one cooking. "How will your pa do without you there to cook and clean?"

Henrietta shrugged. "I guess I'll run up the hill and cook for him for two or three days, and then go back and do it all again. I should be able to have food ready for him for each meal, just by running up a couple of days per week. He can eat the same things over and over. While food is cooking, I can clean the house."

"That sounds like a good plan. Have you talked to your pa about it."

"I mentioned it, but he said he'd cook for himself, and I needed to focus on you once we're married. I've never once seen him cook, but with Ma gone, it's going to be different. He'll need to learn to fix some basic dishes."

"Probably. But I wouldn't mind you helping him out. At least until the children come." His mind was filled with the idea of making the babies, and not having them, but he didn't think that made him a bad person. He had the prettiest girl he'd ever met standing beside him.

"I like the idea of having children with you." In her mind, she was holding a tiny babe, and feeding him. Oh, she loved the idea of having his child.

"Would your father disown you and refuse to let me ever see you again if I kissed you?" he asked, keeping his voice soft so as not to be heard.

"I think he probably would. And then he'd send my brothers to hunt you down and kill you. He's a bit overprotective. He only had one girl you see."

"I understand. What would you say to me kissing you if he wasn't here?"

"I would ask you to wait until we'd been courting longer. Sorry. I feel like a lady shouldn't kiss so quickly."

He sighed. "I suppose you're right." He thought for a moment, trying to come up with something to say after that. "Do you prefer to be called Henrietta or Henri?"

She smiled. "Henri has always been a special nickname my family uses. I'd rather everyone doesn't call me Henri, but it would be nice to hear it from your lips."

"I'll have to call you Henri then. Though Roy marrying Henri doesn't sound like it should be possible..."

Henri giggled. "No, it does not."

He grinned. "Well, considering my father and I dug a cellar today, I should get to my bed...or ground. I don't know when I can see you again. My father is insisting we spend all of our time building, as I'm sure your father is as well."

"He is, but not me of course. Only the boys."

"If I don't see you before then, I'll see you on Sunday during the church raising."

She nodded. "That should be a fun day. We'll all work together to build a cabin large enough to worship in. I think the pastor and Hannah plan to spend the winter in the church."

"I wouldn't be surprised." He squeezed her hand tightly. "I'll see you then, but if I can get away, I'll see you before."

"Maybe I'll pop down and surprise you." Taking him some cookies or a sandwich or two would be an excuse to see him. And she'd just perfected making cookies over a campfire.

"I'd love that," he said, smiling at her.

With that, he hurried away down the hill and to his "bed." It was going to be a long couple of weeks of building if he couldn't see Henri.

When he woke the following morning, Roy shivered and stood up, doing a few jumping jacks to get his body moving. He found gloves and grabbed an axe. Everyone else was still sleeping, but he could see well enough to chop down a few trees. Perhaps his father would let him escape a little early if he worked hard before the others woke.

His father joined him within thirty minutes. "Your mother is making breakfast while your sisters gather the eggs and milk the cows. I thought I'd join you while I wait for them to call us for breakfast."

"Let's see how many trees we can cut down." He'd already cut two. And they were big, long trees they could get plenty of logs out of.

The two of them worked in relative silence. The only sound being the whack of their axes against the tree trunks. They had six trees around them when his mother called them to breakfast.

Sitting for breakfast, he looked at his three sisters. He'd heard several men say that Emma was the prettiest girl in camp, but he just didn't see it. Henrietta was far prettier as far as he was concerned.

Abigail was his second sister, and she wasn't as pretty and a great deal more studious. She was sixteen and had never really had a beau, which he thought was a good thing. None of his sisters had beaus though. He and his father had managed to chase all the young men away.

His youngest sister was Barbara, and she was very flighty in his opinion. She was interested in one thing and then another. She couldn't focus on any one thing, but at twelve, he couldn't really expect her to.

His mind was filled with Henri as they ate and thinking about how much progress they could make on the cabin that day. So much work had to be done, but it was important that it was finished quickly.

Halfway through the meal, he looked at his pa. "Why don't we have Barbara help us with the work today? I think she could be a big help with packing the mud between the logs that will make the floor."

Barbara wrinkled her nose. "That's men's work!"

Pa looked at Barbara. "Your brother's right. You can spend the day helping us along with Abigail. There's too much to do to call anything women's work and men's work. Right now, it's all work, and it must be done quickly."

Though Roy knew his sisters were angry with him, he didn't care. They'd save half a day's work with the two girls helping. Any time they could save was good time.

Ma nodded. "Yes, I think that sounds good. After Emma and I finish the dishes and get something cooking for our noon meal, we'll join you. Many hands make the work light."

Emma glared at Roy then. He smiled back at her sweetly. Having all four of them helping meant they could get the job done without the help of the men. Then he and his father could spend the entire day chopping down trees. They would get a great deal more done with all of them working together.

The floor was mostly in place by the time they sat down for their noon meal, which was potato soup. Roy had always been particularly fond of the soup because it was warm and filled him up, but not making him so full he couldn't work.

After lunch, he and his father worked on the logs, while the ladies all worked on packing the floor. He was sure they could help chink the cabins as well, taking days off the amount of time it would take to build the cabins.

While they were working, he caught a movement out of the side of his eye and saw Henri approaching with a basket. She offered cookies to him and his father. He gratefully took one, knowing it would help his energy stay high for the rest of the day. "This is delicious!"

Henri smiled. "I just figured out how to get cookies to turn out perfectly over an open fire. I had a real oven at home, and I kind of miss it."

"Where was home?" he asked, taking another cookie.

"Indiana. There is so much corn in Indiana. I was happy to see other crops growing during our journey."

He grinned. "We're from Iowa. Lots of corn there as well."

"Would you like a cookie, Mr. Williams?" she asked.

Pa took one of the offered cookies and bit into it. "This is a wonderful cookie. You need to give my wife the receipt."

"I will." Henri looked proud of herself, giving more cookies to the men, and then wandering toward the ladies.

"Keep that one," Pa said. "She's a hard worker if she was willing to climb down that hill to bring you a treat. And she can bake."

Chapter Three

Henri walked toward Roy's mother and sisters. When she reached them, they were all working on chinking the floor. "I'm sorry to interrupt, but I thought you all might like a cookie. Mr. Williams asked me to give you the receipt."

Mrs. Williams looked up at Henri and smiled. "I hear my boy is courting you."

Henri nodded. "He is. He's sweet."

"You're right about that. Girls, let's wash our hands and we'll try the cookies."

The five of them sat on a blanket that Henri brought along, hoping Roy would have some time to sit with her.

As they all tried her cookies, Mrs. Williams smiled. "I suppose I won't need to worry about whether you're a good enough cook for my son, will I?"

Henri laughed. "You don't need to worry about that at all. Are you all chinking the floor? I would love to help for an hour or two before I go back to cook supper for my family." She'd already baked four loaves of bread, and she would just make a thick soup for supper. They were all working in much colder conditions than they had planned.

"That would be wonderful," Mrs. Williams said. "Are you sure your family doesn't need you?"

"My father doesn't let me help with *any* of the men's work. He said no one helps me clean or do the wash, so I shouldn't be helping them. Besides we have four men to do the work. Two of my brothers are content to share a cabin this winter, and the third brother wants his own. So that means four men building only three cabins."

"That sounds easier than what we're doing," Emma complained. "I don't want to have to get so dirty doing this," she said, waving a hand at the half-finished floor.

"Oh, but won't it be nice when it's all done, and you can look at it and say, 'I helped build my family's cabin.'"

Emma shrugged. "I guess. But my hands will be covered with sores tomorrow. Who will want to court me with my hands looking ugly?"

Mrs. Williams shook her head at her daughter. "The men who have made this trip don't expect their women to have clean and uncalloused hands. They understand that true work leaves its mark. I'm sure every man in our settlement would prefer that you have marked up hands."

Henri nodded. "You should look at my hands. Very calloused. I even took one of my brothers axes this morning and chopped down a small tree for firewood, and I then split the wood myself. I think being someone who will work is so much more important than being someone with pretty hands."

"I never thought of it that way," Emma said. "Now what can you tell me about your oldest brother?"

Henri laughed. "He's a good man. A hard worker. Someone who will make a wonderful husband and father one day."

Emma smiled. "Now that's the kind of information I was looking for."

Henri worked with the women for a full two hours before heading back to her father's camp and putting soup on to go with the bread. Her brothers seemed to go through a lot of bread, and she would keep making anything they would eat so they could work faster.

At supper, she served the soup, bread, and cookies. "I baked cookies today as well as bread," she said.

Bastian grinned, nodding. "It's all delicious. I'm going to need five dozen of these cookies for myself by Sunday."

Henri shook her head. "I could make six dozen for the church raising though. But then you'll have to share."

He sighed dramatically. "You should be baking things that you know I love just for me," he said, frowning at her.

"Find yourself a wife if that's what you want. I'll teach her to bake my cookies."

Pa changed the subject then. "We chopped enough logs for the floor and walls of our cabin today. More than enough if truth be told. Tomorrow we'll dig the cellar, and Saturday, we'll lay the floor and chink it."

"I could chink it, Pa. I was helping the Williams family with their floor chinking today."

Her pa narrowed his eyes at her. "You weren't raised to do men's work."

"I know I wasn't, but Roy's mother and sisters were doing men's work, so I joined them. We had a lot of fun." She looked at her brother Jared. "I do believe Emma Williams is sweet on you."

Jared smiled. "I thought so. I'll have to talk to her pa about courting her soon. But I won't marry her until my cabin is built."

"You should talk to him at the church raising on Sunday."

"I hate that we have to miss an entire day of work for the church raising, but I guess we wouldn't be working on the Sabbath anyway."

"At this time of year, I think we would. God isn't going to be angry if we make shelter for our families," Bastian said.

"Very true," Pa said.

"I'll bake cookies for that day. What else should I make?" Henri asked.

"Venison stew?" Samuel asked. "You make venison stew better than anyone I know."

"I'm happy to make it, but someone has to get a deer tomorrow if I'm going to."

Bastian nodded. "I'll hunt in the morning. I could use a little relaxation."

Henri shook her head. Only her brother would think using a rifle to kill a deer would be relaxing. Thankfully they lived in an area where there were lots of deer.

Early the next morning, Bastian walked into camp with the deer wrapped around his shoulders like a scarf. Sam ran to help him tie the deer upside down in a tree.

Henri smiled. "Now I can make venison stew. I'll make a huge pot." It would be fun to go to the church raising, and Henri was looking forward to it. She wondered if she could band with the Williams ladies, and they could work on chinking together. "Before you all go off to work after breakfast, could someone tote a few buckets of water to me. I need to do the wash."

Samuel nodded. "Sure. Jared and I can do that since Bastian got the deer so quickly."

"Thank you! I'll wash everything, including our Sunday best. Maybe Bastian could string a clothesline for me between the wagon and the closest tree."

Bastian nodded. "I'd be happy to."

Pa yawned. "We're digging the cellar today, so I expect everyone to help me with it."

"We will, Pa," Jared assured him.

As soon as they'd had their eggs and bacon for breakfast, Samuel and Jared fetched water for her, and Bastian tied the clothesline. Pa sat resting a little longer before they started. His boys could do a lot more work than he could. That was certain.

Henri gathered all the laundry that needed washing and got out two huge pots. One for wash water, and one for rinsing. She pulled the scrub board from the back of the wagon. Wash days were the hardest for her since her mother had passed. They'd often cooked together but she and her mother had always done the wash together, and it was strange to do it on her own.

As soon as her brothers were back from the creek, she put a pot onto the campfire for wash water. Then she'd do the rinse water, and she'd wash the dishes with whatever was left.

Her brothers and her pa spent the entire morning digging the cellar, and then they laid out the logs for the floor. "Please let me help with the chinking, Pa," Henri said. "One more pair of hands can only make the process go faster." She shivered as she offered.

Pa nodding grudgingly. "I guess you can. We need to get you in a nice warm cabin as soon as we can. You're not as big as the rest of us, and you don't stay warm like we do. We probably should have stayed in Oregon City for the winter."

"But then we wouldn't be in Clover Creek starting our lives!" Henri would have been sad if they'd stayed in Oregon City and had to pay to stay. Here, they were on their own land, and were able to stay for free.

Pa smiled at her. "But your ma would still be with us." He still had a sadness in his eyes that made Henri want to cry every time she saw it. He would be alone for a long time, if not for the rest of his life.

"I know, Papa. I wish she were here too. There are so many chores that feel like she should be beside me when I do them." Henri walked to her father and wrapped her arms around him. "I wish I could bring her back for you."

"So do I, Henri. So do I."

Working together with her brothers and father wasn't nearly as much fun as working with the Williams ladies. The four of them had laughed and joked the entire time, telling silly stories about things that had happened on the trail.

The men were a great deal quieter and more focused on the job than the other group had been. Henri wasn't certain if men were naturally quieter while they worked, or they'd just run out of things to say to one another.

Her family had always loved spending time together, and it seemed as if they'd had too much of togetherness.

They were finished with the chinking by suppertime, and Pa smiled at Henri. "We wouldn't have gotten it done today without you."

"I'll go fix supper for us."

"We'll be in the woods, chopping more trees. I think we can get some walls on this cabin tomorrow," Pa said with pride in his eyes.

As the four men traipsed off into the wooded area beside them, Henri started a simple supper. They'd all grown fond of johnny cakes on the trail, so she made johnny cakes with bacon and eggs for supper. It was a filling meal that didn't cost much and was quick to make. She knew her father and brothers would be happy coming home to anything she cooked.

She looked around her. She was already thinking of Clover Creek as home, and they didn't even have walls. This plot of land was going to be a great place to live. She just hoped her pa remembered she wanted her window overlooking the whole valley. What better way to wash dishes than to look at something beautiful while she did?

While they were finishing up supper, Roy joined them. "You have more cookies?" he asked, looking around.

Henri shook her head. "No, Bastian ate them all!"

"Well, that wasn't very nice."

"I'll bake a bunch more for the church raising," she said softly.

"I'd like that a lot."

"I'll fight you for them!" Bastian said.

Pa shook his head. "No fighting over cookies on my watch." He looked at Roy. "How's your cabin coming?"

"We're working on my family's cabin first, and we started on the walls today. We'll have to chop more wood in the morning, but I think we can have a roof on it by the end of next week." Roy looked at their cabin. "Are you starting on walls tomorrow?"

"We are. We have the wood we need for this cabin and then one more. We've been chopping and trying to get most of that done, and then we'll finish this first cabin and start the second. We're only doing one cellar, so the other two should go up faster."

Roy smiled. "That sounds good to me. Won't it be nice when we can all sleep indoors again?" As he talked, he moved his hands just enough that his arm brushed against Henri's. "Henri helped with our floor yesterday. She did a great job chinking it with my mother and sisters."

"Yeah, she did a good job for us today, too!" Pa said. "I was impressed that she could work that hard."

Henri laughed softly. "You think chinking is hard work? Let me introduce you to laundry."

Roy looked at her for a moment, trying to decide if she was joking. He saw the deer hanging not far from camp. "Oh, that's a big one. Who got the buck?"

"I did," Bastian said. "I want Henri to make her venison stew for the church raising, so I had to get her a good-sized deer."

He gaped at the sheer size of the animal. "Would you use it all for one meal?"

Henri shook her head. "No, I'll use some for the church raising, and I'll dry some for the winter when it's hard to hunt."

"That sounds smart. I just can't imagine that much meat used for one meal."

"Well, it's possible, but I only need to take the amount of food that would feed my family." But she'd take more. Her mother had always taught her to make at least half again as much as she thought she would need. Then she would never have too little. "I may salt a little of it. Then I can make stew again."

Bastian nodded emphatically. "I don't know how or why, but Henri's a better cook than our ma was."

"I'm more creative with seasonings. That's all." Henri didn't want anyone to think she was better than her ma at anything.

She pulled the cake she'd made while waiting for the clothes to dry out of the back of the wagon and served everyone a piece.

Roy's eyes lit up as soon as he saw the cake. Her brother Jared took the first bite. "Oh, this is terrible. Don't even try it. I'll take care of the whole cake, so Henri doesn't have to be embarrassed."

Roy looked at his cake, then looked at her pa and all her brothers who were eating as fast as they could, and he knew better. He took a small bite, and a smile crossed his face. "This is delicious, Henri."

"Thank you. My brothers always try to get the whole desserts by saying it's awful. If they say that, it means it's delicious." Henri rolled her eyes at her brothers' antics.

"I'll keep that in mind. I can't believe you can bake this well!" Roy was thrilled to be getting a woman who could cook and who wasn't afraid of hard work. Well, he hoped he'd be getting her. He had to have that cabin built first. "Did all of you get your own land?"

Bastian answered for everyone. "We did. We're building one huge ranch. All of us will work for it, and we'll split profits."

"That sounds good. I'm doing the same with my pa. We're excited to get started."

"We are too!" Samuel said. "I can't wait until spring when we'll have calves. I know it will be Henri's favorite time of year. She loves baby animals."

"I do," Henri said. "I like human babies as well."

"That's probably good," Bastian said with a grin. "I don't know what we'd do with you if you hated babies."

"Stop!" she said to Bastian, knowing he never would. She just didn't want him to tease her in front of Roy.

Roy grinned at her. "They're your brothers. They're supposed to tease you."

"Do you tease your sisters?" she asked.

"Well, sure, but there's only one of me and three of them. I don't think I could ever tease them as much as you get teased."

"That's true. We're both outnumbered by our siblings."

Samuel looked at Roy. "I hope you're not planning to steal our sister from us. We need to eat!"

"I'll teach each of you to cook one meal. Then you will have four meals you can make, and you can rotate them." Henri knew they'd protest, but she thought it was a good idea.

"That's not a terrible idea," Pa said. "I think every man should be able to cook a meal or two."

Jared looked at his father. "You can cook?"

Pa nodded. "I can cook pancakes and I know how to make a meat and gravy, and mashed potatoes. I could live the rest of my life on what I know how to cook."

"So, I'll teach each of you to make a breakfast, and each of you to make a supper. One person can cook each day, and what's left can be served for the noon meal the next day."

"We're going to take you up on that," Pa said. "Teach each of us to cook two meals, and we'll feed ourselves all winter."

"Who do I get to teach laundry to?" she asked.

Bastian shook his head. "Forget that. You're doing our laundry until your dying day."

Chapter Four

Roy and his father had some of the walls up by Saturday evening. They'd even gotten the loft built. The only thing left to do was roof it, but they had shelter as it was with the loft there. The walls for the loft weren't yet up, but they could make that happen the following week.

Sunday was the church raising. A week from Monday they would be able to start on Roy's cabin. It was supposed to take longer than that to build a cabin, but they both worked from sunup to sundown, and they had worked as hard as they could, doing everything the way they thought was most efficient.

His ma wasn't thrilled with how small the cabin was, but she knew Pa would be building her a house next summer. If he could do it around ranching, of course. But Roy was certain they could do it before and after ranching. They were used to hard work.

His house would probably have to wait a full year, but that was all right with him. He and Henri wouldn't need a lot of space anyway.

There was no stove, so Ma would have to cook in their fireplace, which she and her daughters had helped with, but she was used to cooking over an open fire now.

When he woke Sunday, Roy was excited. Yes, he'd still be building, which wasn't his favorite thing, but they would be building with friends, and he would get to see Henri all day. It would be wonderful!

His family drove to the church together. It wasn't far, and they certainly could have walked, but it was nice not to have to. When they arrived at the church building, He jumped from the back of the wagon and took some of the food his mother had brought to share. Nothing would be hot by the time lunch rolled around, but that was fine with him. He still got to see Henri.

He was already working to help stack the rocks for the fireplace when he spotted Henri with her entire family. The boys all jumped out of the back, and Bastian walked around to help her down. Then she distributed food for her brothers to carry inside. Bastian carried a huge pot and put it on the table where they were setting the food. It was covered, but he sure hoped it was her venison stew. His mouth was already craving it.

Henri came to him with a basket and handed him one of her cookies. He grinned at her. "I hope you brought a lot."

"Oh, trust me, I did. I made two dozen to stay at home, six dozen for the community, and two dozen for me to walk around feeding anyone I want to feed. You know, like you."

Roy grinned. "I think courting you may be one of the smartest things I've ever done."

She smiled. "I sure hope so! One more cookie before I offer to others?"

"I would like that. Thank you for thinking of me."

"Oh, don't worry. I never stop thinking of you." Giving him another cookie, she wandered over to his father and offered him a couple.

"If my son doesn't marry you, I'm going to adopt you so you can bake for me every day." Mr. Williams grinned at her.

Henri laughed at that. "I suppose we could do that, but I think I'd rather just marry your son." She held out the basket. "One more before I move on?"

"Absolutely."

Henri had never been one to really involve herself in the things the others were doing along the trail, and right then, she could see she'd made a mistake. There were kind loving people whom she hadn't even bothered to get to know. She would need to now that they were all settling together.

She walked around the floor of the church, which had been accomplished that week, and she offered each man working a cookie or two. When she was finished, she sought out Roy's sisters and mother.

"Hello, Mrs. Williams. Emma, Abigail, Barbara." Henri smiled sweetly at the women she hoped would be her in-laws very soon.

"What's in the basket?" Mrs. Williams asked. "My husband said he'll never speak to me again if I don't get the receipt for the cookies, you made the other day."

Henri giggled. "That's what's in the basket, and your husband has already had three."

Mrs. Williams sighed. "If I didn't know how hard he was working today, I would scold you for ruining his lunch, but I do know he's going to need snacks throughout the day, and he'd prefer your cookies to the jerky I brought."

"I really do need to make sure all of you ladies can make these cookies." Henri looked at Emma. She needed to be the first person she taught, as she had a feeling she would soon be married to Jared.

"We'd love to learn," Emma said softly. Henri had noticed that when there were men around, she was always soft spoken. When the men weren't there though, she was loud and boisterous. Henri was glad she didn't have to decide how to be in any situation. She was always just herself.

"What are the women doing to help?" Henri asked, knowing that the others had been there longer than she had.

"Chinking, and that's about all. We'll serve the noon meal, and we all brought food. I think we're just supposed to mingle for the most part."

Hannah, Pastor Jed's wife, wandered over to them. "How are your homes coming along?"

Mrs. Williams smiled and nodded. "We're staying indoors now. The men will finish the walls on Monday, we hope, but they built a loft for the girls to sleep in, so we have something over our heads."

"Oh, that's wonderful!" Hannah said before turning her attention to Henri. "And you, Henrietta?"

"The first cabin has some walls. Just a little more chinking, which I've been doing rather than take any of the men away from the work. Bastian and Sam plan to share a cabin, so theirs will be the next they work on, but Pa thinks it'll be mid-week before he can even start on theirs, and then Jared hopes to be married before winter sets in. So after they do Sam and Bastian's, they'll build Jared's. What about yours?"

"We've decided to just build a bigger church for now, and Jed and I will live in a room partitioned off from the rest. The fireplace on the other side of the church is where I'll be doing my cooking."

"That sounds good," Mrs. Williams said. "I'm glad you'll have a roof over your head this winter, especially with the baby coming."

Hannah patted her burgeoning stomach. "The baby is what matters."

"I couldn't agree more," Henri said. She was so excited at the idea of having babies, it was hard to think of anything else.

"My kitten just had her first litter. Would any of you like a kitten to be a mouser? I'm sure we're going to get a lot of mice from these fields all around us."

"I would," Henri said quickly. Her father wasn't a fan of kittens, but she had a feeling she could convince Roy it was a good idea to keep the mice away.

"Great. I'll introduce you to them later, and you can choose your favorite. They won't be ready to go for six weeks or so, but I want them to go to people who will love them."

"I will love a kitten. So much!" Henri wanted to jump up and down with excitement.

"After the men are done building the fireplaces, we women will be chinking. Do you all know how to do that?" Hannah asked.

All five of them nodded. "I learned from Mrs. Williams and her daughters." Henri had to give credit where it was due.

"I heard Roy was courting you...is it true?"

Henri blushed but nodded. "He is."

"I hoped it was true, and I wasn't causing a problem by listening to gossip. I prefer to know if what I've been told is true or not." Hannah smiled at Henri as she left the small group and moved on to the next group of ladies.

Henri smiled. "I do think she's going to be the best pastor's wife in the whole world."

Mrs. Williams nodded. "She's sweet, and she's always willing to help however she can. I know that Jed is proud of her. I hope she's still able to do what she needs to do when the babes start coming."

"I think she will," Henri said. "She's never been one to shirk hard work."

Emma immediately changed the subject. "I see your brother Jared," she said to Henri. "Ma, do we have any treats I can offer him?"

Mrs. Williams nodded. "We do. I brought my buffalo jerky that we made on the trail. I've been complimented on the spices I use many times. It will be good for keeping energy up."

"Oh, good! Where is it?" Emma asked.

"In a basket in the back of the wagon. Make sure you offer it to all the men and not just Jared. He doesn't need to know you're sweet on him."

Henri hid a smile. Her brother was just as sweet on Emma as she was on him. "I'm sure he'll be thrilled to have something to snack on while he works."

Soon, Hannah came to them and assigned the group of ladies to one of the fireplaces. "You said you know how to chink. We have some mud mixed up in a bucket beside each of the two fireplaces."

Henri was thrilled she could be of use, thanks to the Williams ladies. Walking to the fireplace Roy had been working on, she smiled at him as he went to a new task. He turned and watched her walk away, causing him to stumble into his father.

"Roy, get your mind off the girl and on your work. You can't be distracted on a work site." His father shook his head. "What are you thinking, boy?"

Roy was a little surprised his father didn't cuff him on the side of his head. He deserved it. Both men went to help with getting the logs for the walls ready. There would be one window in the pastor's quarters. They joked that it was so people wouldn't be distracted during church, but they all knew the truth. It took more time to cut out windows, and it was time they didn't have if they wanted all the building done before it snowed. Besides none of them had glass for windows, so they were just covering them with oilcloth, which could be rolled up out of the way when you needed air or wanted to look out.

When it was time for lunch, the ladies all stood with their own meals, and Roy looked up and down the line for Henri. As he watched her, she removed the lid from her pot, and he could see that it was indeed a stew, and he could only pray it was venison.

Each family had brought their own bowls, utensils, and plates that they could wash at home later, after the work was done, so as soon as the prayer was over, he hurried over to Henri. "The food looks delicious. And you look beautiful."

She laughed, holding up her arm where some mud had landed on the old dress she'd chosen to work in. "I look ridiculous. I need a bath."

He smiled. "I like it when you're a little messy."

Blushing, she shook her head. "You're a silly man, Roy Williams."

He shrugged at her. "Is this the venison stew Bastian couldn't quit talking about?"

"Yes, it is. I made more for home, and I even made you a little pot of your own if you like it. If not, I'm certain Bastian will eat it all for you."

"I'm sure he would, but he's not getting the opportunity." He looked around and realized he was holding up the line, "Oops, I'd better let other people try your stew."

She smiled as he walked in one direction down the line, but she knew he'd missed out on some delicious meals when he'd walked straight to her rather than go down the entire line as he was supposed to.

Henri stayed where she was, scooping up generous portions of stew for the men who came through the line. There was little left when it was time for the women to eat, and she wanted to sample some of the other women's cooking not her own. So, she fetched the tableware she'd brought for herself, and went through the line to try things that were left over.

Once her plate was filled, she found her way to Roy, who had saved a spot for her on the bench where he was sitting. "Where did these come from?" she asked.

"While most of the men are working on the church, there's a small group working on making pews for the church. They're just going to be made from logs for now, but it's a place to sit. Most of the benches are done after the work put in this morning, and then those men will be able to help build the walls."

"Do you think you'll be able to get the roof on today?" she asked, looking at the clouds that looked like they were about to dump a lot of rain or snow on them. She was thankful her father and brothers had worked so hard to get the walls mostly up on the cabin. With the loft in place, she would have shelter from the rain even before the roof was on.

"I think we will. There are too many of us working not to."

"That'll be good. Hannah doesn't need to get sick this close to her due date."

"I love this stew. If you really made a small pot just for me, I'll take it. My father will soon be insisting that you teach my mother and sisters all your receipts. I think your stew is all he got." He spooned another bite of stew into his mouth.

"No, I saw him get biscuits too." She hoped his father enjoyed the food. In her mind, his father could tell him not to marry her if her cooking wasn't good enough. Roy obviously thought it was good. He had a little line of stew on his chin, but she didn't tell him. She thought he looked adorable with the food she'd cooked in the middle of his beard.

Roy looked over at her as she ate food his mother had made. "What do you think?"

She shrugged. "It's pretty good."

"Do you make a potato soup?" It was one of his favorite things, and if she didn't make one, she'd have to learn from his mother.

"I do. Mine is different, but I do make one."

He leaned close and whispered, "Is it better than Ma's?"

"I wouldn't say that!" she said, though hers was *much* better. She was almost happy that his mother wasn't a wonderful cook, because it made her look so much better.

"I have a feeling it is better. You're a wonderful cook, but my ma is just mediocre. I didn't realize how little talent she had for cooking until I went on the trail and sampled other meals."

"Don't say that to her, please! She doesn't need to have her cooking compared to mine. My brothers all told Ma they liked my food better, and she was sad for a few days. Then she decided she'd just be proud that her daughter was a good cook."

"I won't say anything to her about it." He looked over at her and couldn't help but fall a little more in love with her. She was so special to him already. "As soon as I finish my cabin, I plan to ask your pa for your hand."

Her smile seemed to light up the gloomy day. "I would adore that. And Pa says I'm to teach my brothers to each cook a breakfast and a dinner. Then they can all take turns cooking, and I don't have to do it."

"I think that's a great idea. Pa and I are going to start on my cabin a week from Monday, if we can stay on schedule. So far, it's going much faster than we expected."

"How long do you think it will take you?" she asked, looking forward to calling the man beside her husband.

"My cabin isn't going to be nearly as big as Ma and Pa's. We'll use their cellar for the storage we need, so we don't have to dig a cellar. We don't need a loft because we don't have children. Even if we had a baby by the end of summer, we sure wouldn't be putting it in the loft!"

"Very true." Henri was so excited at the thought of marrying him. "If you need help with the chinking, just let me know. I've found I really enjoy it."

"Ma and the girls will probably chink our cabin. We're all working together on both," he said. "You just teach those brothers of yours to cook!"

"I plan to."

He frowned for a moment. "I just realized that if Emma and Jared marry, he is not going to be happy with her cooking. She's not as good as Ma."

"I'd be happy to teach her to make all his favorite dishes," she said. "I'm looking forward to having sisters."

"I have to say, I look forward to the idea of brothers."

A bell rang, and they both knew it was time to get back to work. She wished they'd had more time to sit alone together in a crowd. They could have a private conversation, but her pa wasn't worried they would do something they shouldn't.

She put her plate into the back of the wagon, with Pa's and her brothers'. She'd wash them that evening. For now, it was time to get back to work on their house of worship.

Chapter Five

Roy visited for at least a few minutes every day. He and Henri sat together in church two Sundays later, and she invited him to supper. "I'd like that."

"We eat at six."

"I'll be there." He looked up and down the row to see if anyone was looking at them, and he squeezed her hand. He didn't know why he worried because the entire community knew they were courting, but to hold her hand in church? He just wasn't sure if that was proper.

Henri was thankful that the cabin was finally built. Her father and brothers were still building every day, but she'd done what she could to make the house cozy. There were curtains at the one window that looked out over the valley, which was in her "kitchen."

The entire kitchen was the fireplace she used for cooking, a basin, and a table and benches. The table and benches were what her brothers had built for her in the evenings. One of the legs on the table was a little shorter than the others, so she had a wad of linen tucked under it to keep it stable. They'd even sanded the benches so no one would get splinters by sitting on them.

Her loft was comfortable with a mattress on the floor. She hoped she wouldn't be living up there long, but she knew she may. As she made supper that evening, she kept thinking about how it would be the first time Roy had eaten an entire meal she'd cooked.

She made ten loaves of bread. As the bread was rising, she cut out dumplings for chicken and dumplings. It was the one meal she'd craved more than any other on the trail. Bastian had done an afternoon's worth of work for a neighbor, who had paid him in chickens, so she was able to cook the dish she loved so much.

Her father and brothers were out building the cabin for Samuel and Bastian. They would start on Jared's as soon as Sam and Bastian's was done. Jared was only one person for the third cabin, so he had to wait while they built the other two.

She had already cooked the chicken and deboned it. She'd never been a fan of deboning chicken, but she certainly knew how. As she worked, she heard the door open behind her. Glancing over her shoulder, she saw it was just Bastian. "Where are the others?"

"I wasn't feeling quite right, so I came back here early."

"Do you need me to do anything for you? I could brew some willow bark tea."

"What will that do?" he asked.

"The Indians use it to bring down fevers."

Bastian nodded. "All right. I'll drink the tea."

That's when she knew he wasn't feeling well. Her mother had taught her a trick for when her brothers and pa were sick. Offer them some medicine. If they accepted it, they were truly sick and felt terrible. If not, then they were exaggerating their symptoms. It was simple, and she knew it would help her when she had children of her own.

She heated some water in the metal coffee pot and then poured it into a mug for him, over the willow bark leaves. She didn't know where her mother had heard of the remedy, but she was glad she knew how to make it. And they'd collected medicinal herbs all the way along the trail. Her ma had been much better with medicines than any other woman she knew.

While Bastian drank his tree and ate the cookie she gave him, she started making the bread. She made it in an iron skillet which made it look strange, but over an open fire, it was the best way to bake bread.

After the bread was done, she put the broth from boiling the chicken earlier and the chicken back over the fire. As soon as it was boiling again, she dropped in her dumplings.

Bastian groaned. "That smells so good." He sniffled. "I can't believe I can smell it through this messed up nose of mine, but I can, and I can't wait to eat my share."

Henri grinned. "I'm glad you love my chicken and dumplings so much that you worked for these chickens."

"Oh, please. We were all wanting it the whole time we were on the trail. Ma made good chicken and dumplings, but there's just something you do that makes them taste so much better."

"I hate when you compare me to Ma. She was better than me in every way, and I'll always fall short."

Bastian slowly shook his head. "You've always been better in the kitchen than ma. Sure, she made her remedies that did help us, but she couldn't cook anywhere near as well as you do. And I'm sure you can make all the remedies now as well."

"Ma made me a receipt book of her remedies. I will always treasure it." She seemed to feel so much more about their mother's death than anyone else in the family. She wasn't sure if it was because she was the only daughter or because the men hid their feelings.

Just before six, there was a knock at the door. She hurried to open it seeing Roy standing there, hat in hand. "Am I too late?"

She smiled. "I'm just about to put supper on. I need to warn you, Bastian is feeling a little under the weather."

Roy shook his head. "I'm not worried." He would risk getting sick if it meant more time with Henri.

She opened the door wider so he could come inside, and he looked around the cabin. "This is nice!"

Bastian nodded. "We built it with our own eight hands."

Roy's lips quirked. "Whose are you building next?" He sat down on the bench opposite Bastian.

"Mine and Sam's. Jared has to wait cuz he's only one person."

"Well, he is courting my sister."

"He is. But he still must wait. Sometimes you must not be first at everything."

Roy grinned. "I can see that." He shook his head. "As the oldest, my sisters complain that I do everything first all the time."

Bastian nodded. "But I'm happy to say that my sister was making my favorite food already, and it's good for when you're sick."

"Something smells really good!" Roy said, looking at Henri standing over a pot and stirring. "What is it?"

"Chicken and dumplings. One of our neighbors in Indiana was from the south, and she had always had them. Ma got the receipt and then she taught me," Henri said.

"But Henri's are better than Ma's," Bastian said.

Henri gave her brother a look, letting him know that she didn't appreciate the comparison to her mother at all.

Her father and other two brothers came into the house then, and Roy stood up. "May I speak to you alone, sir?"

Pa looked exhausted, but he nodded and stepped right back outside. Henri wished she could hear what the two men were saying, but they'd made the cabin too well. She couldn't hear a single word. She thought about rolling back the oilcloth from her window, so she could hear them, but she knew better. Pa would not be happy with her.

By the time Roy and Pa came back into the house, she had supper on the table. She'd sliced the shallow loaves of bread and put out fresh butter for it. And there were bowls filled with her chicken and dumplings.

Roy sat beside Henri, and her brothers kept giving him goofy grins. Bastian looked like he was going to say something rude at one point, so Henri kicked him under the table.

"Ow! Don't kick me. I'm sick!"

"Sick in the head," she mumbled.

Roy chuckled but didn't say anything. He was enjoying the family dynamic a great deal. It was always fun to eat with someone else's family and see how they did things. This family seemed to make jokes a great deal more than his did.

As soon as supper was over, Roy got to his feet. "Would you walk with me?" he asked Henri.

She frowned, looking at all the dishes she still needed to do.

"You can do the dishes when you get back," Pa said. "Walk with Roy."

She was surprised to hear Pa say that. Usually, he was against her being alone with Roy even for a moment. "Yes, Pa." She wanted to walk with Roy, but she knew the dishes would be harder to wash the longer she waited.

She grabbed her coat and followed him outside, surprised at how very cold it was at night. It was much warmer during the day.

Roy took her hand and walked around the side of the house with her because he knew her family wouldn't be able to see them there. "I just asked for your hand in marriage, and your pa said yes. My cabin is finished, and we can marry as soon as you're ready."

Henri grinned. "Are you going to ask me?"

Roy chuckled. "Henri, will you be my wife?"

"I would be honored." She stepped toward him and raised her lips for his kiss. Maybe her pa wouldn't approve, but kissing should be all right when they'd decided to marry.

Roy didn't think twice, wrapping his arms around her and kissing her softly. "How would you feel about going to the church in the morning and getting Pastor Jed to marry us?"

"That would make me very happy. I've already taught my brothers to make two meals each, so they should be mostly self-sufficient. I will probably still have to bake bread for them."

"That's fine. You know I don't mind if you see to your family's needs. We've already talked about it."

"I know. I just feel like I should be a full-time wife and not a part-time daughter, so I wanted to make certain you were all right with it." Henri was glad he didn't seem to have a problem with it.

"You are doing what you need to do for your family."

"I feel like I always will."

"That's fine. I wouldn't even mind if you made them supper a couple of nights per week to help out."

"I may do that," she said.

"I'll pick you up in my wagon tomorrow around ten. Will that give you enough time to see to your chores first?"

She nodded. "I'll bake lots more bread for them, and probably even have supper going. They'll be much happier if we ease them into things." Inside she was floating on air. Finally, she was going to marry Roy Williams. She loved him and nothing was going to stop her.

He walked her back to the front door, kissing her one more time before leaving. "I'll see you in the morning."

"I can't wait to be your wife," she said softly.

When she walked into the house a minute later, her pa asked, "When's the wedding?"

"He's picking me up at ten tomorrow morning. I'll make bread in the morning before I go, and I'll make a thick stew for you to reheat for supper. Will that help you?"

Pa nodded. "I don't think I'm quite ready to eat something one of these three has learned to cook."

"If you eat with your eyes closed, you won't see how burnt it all is," Henri recommended.

That earned her a glare from Bastian, who seemed to be feeling better after the willow bark tea and the meal. "I can make what you showed me. I'm going to be the best cook around!"

Henri simply smirked at him, not willing to argue.

She quickly washed the dishes with the water she'd put on to heat before supper. When she finished, she hung her apron on a peg on the wall. She had thought about packing it for her move to Roy's cabin, but it made more sense to keep it out for when she cooked supper in the morning.

"I'm going to put myself to bed," she said. It was already after eight, and there were things she felt like she must do before she could marry her sweetheart.

"G'night!" Pa called. Her brothers echoed their father.

"Sleep sweet!" she called as she climbed the ladder. "I love you all!"

When she got upstairs, she changed into her nightgown, and pulled her best dress from her pile of dresses. There were only four, so it wasn't hard to find.

She packed the other dresses, including the one she'd been wearing, and made sure she was leaving nothing behind. She wished she had a trunk, but there wasn't one, so she made do with a pillowcase. She'd had a trunk in Indiana, but it had been too heavy for the oxen to pull and it would take up precious space they needed for food.

As she climbed into bed, she closed her eyes and dreamed about how blissful married life would be. She could already see herself with a baby in her arms. Life would be wonderful.

*****

She woke before the sun the following morning, as was her habit. She carried the pillowcase with all her belongings downstairs with her, and then she hurriedly mixed up a huge batch of bread dough.

While the dough was rising, she started a fire in the fireplace, and started on a stew for supper the next night. Bastian had gotten another deer on Saturday, so she was able to make a huge pot that would last for at least a couple of days.

While the stew cooked for a while, she mixed up pancake batter. Everyone would be pleased with her pancakes before Sam started making his. She had a feeling Sam would let them burn every time.

She was just taking the stew out of the fireplace and putting the pancakes in when Bastian came out. She looked at him. "How are you feeling?"

He shrugged. "Not great but not too bad either."

"Would you like me to make you some more willow bark tea?"

"No, thanks. I don't feel bad enough for it."

Henri smiled. "Good. You're planning to work today?"

"I am. I want to move out of this tiny cabin into the tiny cabin I'll share with Sam. Of course, with you gone, I could just stay in your loft."

"You're welcome to it. I'll be living happily ever after in the cabin that Roy built for both of us."

Bastian nodded. "Who should I marry?" he asked.

Henri shook her head. "Why would you think I had an answer to that question?"

"You know the women in the company better than I do."

"That may be true, but I still can't decide whom you should marry. I can't see inside your head."

"There has to be someone..."

Henri sighed. "Perhaps you should look around at church on Sunday and see if any of the young ladies suit your fancy. I'd be happy to introduce you as soon as you were ready."

"That doesn't sound like a bad idea. I'll try that."

"Good," she said, turning her attention back to the pancakes. The first four were done, so she put them on a plate and started the next four. Bastian was all too willing to grab the four of them and add butter and syrup.

She continued to cook until her other two brothers and her father came out of the bedroom. All four of them had been sleeping there. She knew when she left, her brothers really would take over her loft.

After making herself a couple of pancakes, she sat at the table with her family. "I will bake bread before I go. I have already mixed up a stew and started it cooking. I would wait and put it in the fireplace around five this evening if you want it to be hot. There's plenty of fresh butter for all of you. Let me know if you need anything else, and I'll make sure I do it."

Pa looked at her. "Will you still do our laundry? At least until all the cabins are done."

"Of course, I will. I'll come up and do it every Friday, and I'll probably bring our laundry as well."

"That sounds good," Pa said. "It's going to be awful quiet without you here, humming as you go about your work. Just like your ma did."

Henri smiled at her father. "I miss her every day."

Pa nodded. "I know you do. I'm sure she's watching over all of us."

After breakfast, she did the dishes, and then she scrubbed the floors one last time. By the time Roy had arrived, the cabin was in perfect order, and she had a stew slow cooking over the fire. Ten loaves of bread spread out over the table. They wouldn't have to cook for a day or two, and she would bake more bread on Wednesday.

It wouldn't be a difficult chore because she would be baking bread for herself and Roy anyway.

The men were out finishing up the second cabin when Roy picked her up. She put her meager belongings into the back of his wagon. "Are you ready for this?" she asked, her eyes filled with excitement.

"Definitely," he said. "We'll be married before noon."

"We will."

"My ma invited us to have supper with them Friday night. I thought it might be nice for you to have a night off cooking."

She laughed. "I've already baked ten loaves of bread and a huge pot of stew as well as breakfast for my father and brothers. I would love a day off cooking soon."

He chuckled. "Ma's trying to make it so you don't have to cook. I guess that's just not possible."

"I love cooking. Maybe your ma is someone who dreads it, but I'd rather cook than do any other household chore."

"I can understand that. Especially since you're so good at it. Ma loves to sew as much as she hates to cook. At least we all have mended clothes."

"After the trail, I'm surprised any of the clothes we brought from Indiana don't have to be resewn entirely."

While they talked, he drove them down the hill to the church. "The pastor knows we're coming. Mrs. Scott will be there to witness the wedding."

"I'm surprised your ma won't be there."

"She thought it would be insensitive because your ma can't be."

"That's the one thing I miss the most on my wedding day. My mama should be there crying."

Chapter Six

Roy pulled into the churchyard and helped Henri down from the wagon. Walking into the church together made him feel like he was doing something great.

Pastor Scott was ready for them, and Hannah was sitting off to the side of the room, her focus on something else entirely. At least that's how it looked to Henri.

At the front of the church, the two of them stood in front of the pastor. "Are you sure you don't want to wait for family?" Jed asked.

Henri shook her head. "No, I already feel like I shouldn't marry without my mother. If his mother came, I'd feel like I was doing something terribly wrong."

"I can understand that." Jed said a prayer, and then he started the ceremony. "Do you Roy take Henrietta to be your lawfully wedded wife? To love, honor, and cherish for as long as you both shall live?"

"I do," Roy said, his voice eager.

"Do you Henrietta, take Roy to be your lawfully wedded husband. To love, honor, and obey him for as long as you both shall live"

"I do," Henri said, her voice much shakier than Roy's had been.

When Pastor Jed told Roy he could kiss the bride, Roy grabbed her waist and pulled her to him, kissing her. All he could think about was that evening he wouldn't need to stop after one or two kisses. No, he was greatly looking forward to making babies with this girl...his wife.

Roy thanked the pastor and Hannah hurried over to offer her best wishes to Henri. "It seems like this happened very quickly."

"How long did you and the pastor court?" Henri asked.

Hannah laughed. "A day or two."

"And you say that Roy and I went quickly? That's just plain silly." She and Roy had courted for three whole weeks before getting married. It definitely would have been too fast if they'd still been in the east, but the west was something different entirely. Indiana seemed like it was barely a memory at this point.

"It is. I'm sorry about that." Hannah hugged Henri tightly. "Always be true, and no one can ask any more from a wife than that."

"I'll come to you if I have trouble or questions about being a wife," Henri said. "I just wish my mother could have been here today."

"I know her death is still very fresh to you. Perhaps you could think about how happy this marriage would have made her."

Henri thought about that and smiled. Her mother had known how she felt about Roy long before, and she had approved of the match. "Thank you. I will."

On the drive up to his cabin from the church, he couldn't quit grinning. "My cabin is small, but it should be big enough for two, or even three if a third should happen to come along."

"I hope we have a baby right off," Henri said, imagining each tiny finger and toe.

"I hope so too." He wanted children, but he could wait for a year or two with no problem. He liked the idea of spending time alone with his wife before the babies started to come.

"Do you have any food in the cabin?" she asked. "I'll need to cook our noon meal."

"Of course. I have everything my ma told me I'd need. I'll show you when we get there." He wished he'd had time to make a beautiful kitchen for her, but this winter was just about survival. They would be thankful for the roof over their heads. Roy pulled up in front of their small cabin. "I waited until you were here before spending a night. I slept on the floor at my parents' house."

She smiled. "That's sweet. You should have slept where you were more comfortable though."

He helped her down from the wagon, and took her pillowcase from the back, slinging it over one shoulder. He opened the door for her and watched as she looked around. "I'll show you where the food is. Do you want me to start a fire while you look at what we have?"

"That would be wonderful. I love that I'm going to have my own kitchen to cook in."

He grinned. "I do too. I know you're going to make so much food here, and it will all be delicious."

"I do hope so."

He led her to a small area off to the side of the kitchen. "All the food is right there." He gestured to the area. "You should be able to find food to cook for a while."

"Can I talk you into a bit of hunting?" she asked. "We're going to want to have a stockpile of meat while we can get it."

He nodded. "I didn't like venison until you cooked it for me. Now I feel like I would like you to cook it for every meal."

"That's sweet," she said, smiling up at him. When he drew her to him for a kiss, she was a bit startled, but she gladly kissed him back. "Should we kiss during the day? Is that okay?"

"We're going to kiss a lot more than you think. I want you to always know that I'll be by your side."

"All right. You go do whatever you have planned for the day, and I'll get our lunch ready." Looking at what there was to offer, she immediately started devising a meal. She only wished he had fresh meat for her to cook with.

"I was just going to chop some wood before lunch, and then I'll do some hunting this afternoon. I would love to have some fresh meat for you."

"I'd prefer elk or venison to bear, but if you get a bear, make sure to get my father and brothers, and they'll help you with it for a portion of the meat."

"I will. I'd prefer elk or deer or moose myself."

She smiled. "I'm really not a fan of bear meat, but it would last us for a good long while, and we would at least be able to eat through the winter."

"I'm going to be hunting as much as I can through the winter. Pa's and my herds are small enough that we'll put them all in together, and then Pa will take care of them through the winter. I'll hunt for both families. Do you mind that I'm still working so closely with my father?" he asked.

"I'm still doing my family's laundry and making them bread. How could you working with your father bother me?" She shook her head, a smile lighting up her face. "I'm going to make one of my favorite meals from the trail. We'll have jerky with a gravy over rice or mashed potatoes. Do you have a preference?"

He wrinkled his nose. "Rice is always so hard to eat. And it crunches when you eat it."

She frowned. "I'm going to make rice. We'll see if you like it better. It's filling and not very expensive."

"Are you going to be a frugal wife?" He loved the idea of that because they wouldn't hurt for money as often.

"Absolutely. It's my job to be frugal, isn't it?"

Roy walked to her and kissed her. "It is. I'm glad I married you."

Henri wrapped her arms around him in a hug. "I feel the same way."

"Okay. You go get wood chopped, and I'll get our lunch finished."

He headed for the door. "I'll be chopping some every day. We need to have enough for the winter."

"We do!" She couldn't imagine what winter would be like without a great deal of firewood.

Their meal was ready in about an hour, and she went to the door to call him for the meal. "Roy, lunch is ready!"

Roy made one last chop and left the axe in the wood. "I'm coming!"

"Wash your hands," she reminded him. There wasn't a great deal of water for cooking, but they would have to make do. Of course, she could get more water from the creek and boil it, but it was a long way, and she wasn't sure she was strong enough to carry pails full of water that far.

He came in and used a tiny bit of the water, while she put lunch on the table. He looked at the rice and frowned. "I really don't think I'm going to like it this way."

"I'm just as certain you will," she replied. "Do you want coffee?"

He nodded. "I never used to like it, but I got used to it on the trail."

"Me too." The doctor had insisted that any water used for cooking had to be boiled first and they could only drink coffee and tea. She now drank both, but she'd left Indiana drinking neither one.

They sat down together for their first meal as man and wife, and he took her hand in his before praying. He thanked God for the food and for her agreeing to marry him. Everything seemed so perfect to Henri that a single tear traveled down her cheek.

Not only were they in their new home, but they had a roof over their heads, and soon they would have meat for winter. She couldn't ask for more.

Roy took one bite of the rice with the gravy on it—something his mother had made often on the trail—and smiled. "Your rice is so different from my ma's."

"I was hoping you'd like rice when you realized how it's really supposed to taste." She sipped at her coffee.

"My ma really can't cook, can she?"

"I don't want to say anything that would make you think less of your mother. Let's just say that I cook very differently than she does."

"This is delicious. I could eat this every day."

She chuckled. "That's good because we may need to. You have a huge amount of rice there, and I think I want to save most of the potatoes for seed. If I can get you to enjoy rice, it will stretch our food stores a great deal more."

"I'm all for that! Potatoes seem to have been the major crop cultivated by the Indians here."

"Yes, I plan to grow them in my kitchen garden, but I can't do that until spring. Until then, we need to eat what we have." She shook her head. "It's going to be a long hard winter. The more you hunt leading up to the winter, the better off we'll be."

"I agree. All right. I'm happy to eat rice if Ma doesn't make it, and I'll look forward to more potatoes next summer."

She smiled. "I'll choose the ones I want for planting, and we'll still have some for the winter. Just not nearly as many as we'd probably like to have."

"I understand." He was happy she was forward thinking about so many things. She really was going to be a good wife to him. They'd gotten married so quickly, he was a bit worried about how well she'd do at the important tasks of being a wife. The worry left his mind there.

As soon as he was finished eating, he headed out with his rifle to get some game. As much as she preferred other meats, she prayed for a bear. It would keep their family going all winter.

While Roy was gone, Henri did the dishes, and cleaned up the table after their small meal. She looked through what they had left for supper and decided to see if he brought in some game before deciding for certain what to cook. She needed to use fresh meat all she could. Not only did it taste better, but the jerky would be good for later months when there was no fresh meat to be had.

She spent the afternoon sweeping the floors and doing other small tasks to keep their little cabin clean. It was all one room, and there was a bed on the other side of the cabin from her "kitchen." The cabin would be extremely intimate as they got used to one another as newlyweds.

There was no chest to store their clothing in, so she would have to get creative there. She didn't know how skilled Roy was at working with wood, but if he could build either a trunk or a chest for them, it would make her task of keeping their clothes clean much easier.

The floor in the cabin was of course dirt, and while it wasn't her favorite thing to take care of, she knew it would get better. For now, she was just happy to have a roof over her head.

Roy returned after three hours. "I got an elk."

Henri grinned. "That's wonderful! Elks make the best jerky. Do you need someone to help you hang it?" She knew most animals needed to be bled out before they could be used.

He shook his head. "Pa helped me. I promised we'd have them over to supper on Saturday night for the help. And I'll also give them a portion of the meat."

"Of course! I know we'll be sharing meat for a while." She looked out the window and smiled when she saw the sheer size of the elk hanging from a tree twenty yards from her door. "Can you get me a roast from it for supper tonight? After it's drained a little of course."

"I'd be happy to. That sounds really good. With potatoes, carrots, and some of your amazing gravy."

"That's what I'll make then. I'm thankful you like my cooking because it will make things so much easier!"

"Oh, I agree with that. I think I can get a roast for you in about an hour. Does that give you enough time to cook it?" he asked.

"It does. Maybe you should go out and try to find one more. You know you have an hour."

Roy nodded but frowned at the same time. He'd planned to spend their wedding day together, not out hunting. He understood they needed as much food stored as possible, but couldn't that wait until tomorrow? "I'm on my way."

After he was gone, Henri went through the potatoes and chose the ones she thought would be the best to plant in the spring. She put the ones she wanted to grow into a burlap sack and put it aside. The next time they went to his parents' cabin, she'd be sure to ask if she could keep it in their cellar.

She took a few smaller potatoes and peeled and cut them up for their supper, putting them into a huge pot and pouring water over them. Then she peeled some carrots and chopped them, dropping them into the water with the potatoes. An onion was chopped and added to give the whole dish a better flavor.

Now she just had to wait for an elk roast, and she could put it all on for supper. Maybe she could get Roy to go out and get even more game while it cooked.

She realized then she hadn't started the bread for the day. How could she forget bread?

Quickly she mixed up ten loaves as she always had. She didn't think she and Roy would need more than two or three loaves, but she'd take the rest to her father. She'd walk up the hill in the morning.

There was a knock on the door as she was waiting for the bread to rise.

Opening it, she saw Sam and Bastian. "What are you two doing here?" she asked smiling at her brothers.

"We made you a wedding present. We started on it as soon as we realized that you and Roy were courting." Bastian had his usual grin on his face, and she thought about how lucky some girl would be to marry him. Bastian was never in a bad mood, and she was sure that would make marriage much easier.

Henri clapped her hands together. Her brothers were skilled with their hands, and she was sure what they'd brought would be wonderful.

Her brothers stepped out of the way to show her a trunk. It wasn't huge, but it would easily store all their clothes.

"Oh, thank you! I was just thinking I should ask Roy to make me something for our clothes." She hugged both of her brothers in turn.

"We thought this would help. Jared didn't help us with it because he was busy making one of his own. He's courting Emma, you know," Bastian said. Bastian was always the one speaking when it was him and

Sam. Sam was quieter than their brothers, but he had a wonderful sense of humor when he wanted to use it.

"I hadn't heard officially, but I think it's good. Emma is sweet as can be." Henri was truly happy the two of them were dating. It would be nice to have an excuse to spend more time with her new sister-in-law.

"I made ten loaves of bread this morning and left them with Pa. I'm making a bunch more tonight, but I'll come up tomorrow to drop them off. I may even make supper for all of you, but don't count on it. It depends on how busy I'll be."

Bastian nodded. "We understand. We already miss your cooking, but we know you need to cook for your husband now."

"I do," Henri said, looking off in the distance. "Roy seems to be struggling with the game he is bringing in. Would you two make yourselves useful?"

Her brothers hurried off to help Roy. She couldn't tell what kind of animal it was, but she was certain it wasn't a bear. If he could keep bringing in two large animals per day, she was going to be able to dry, or salt, a great deal of meat for winter.

The three men together made short work of the second elk. At least it looked like an elk, and it was almost as big as the one Roy had shot earlier. She wanted to jump up and down and clap her hands, but she was a married woman now, and she therefor needed to be more sedate in the things she did.

Instead, she walked outside to see the men hanging the elk. "You're going to get some incredible meals out of this," Bastian said.

Roy smiled. "I can already taste them."

Chapter Seven

Roy brought her the roast she'd asked for and then carried in the chest her brothers had made for her, setting it at the foot of the bed. "I was planning on making one, but I'm glad I don't have to. It's a very nice wedding gift."

Henri smiled. "I think so too. My brothers tend to spoil me every chance they get."

He could see how very close she was to her family, and he was just as close to his. He hoped there would never be a time they had to choose between parents because it would be hard. "I'm going to go cut a roast for Ma to make for supper as well, but hers will have to be much bigger."

"That's fine. I hope they enjoy it!"

"I think I'm going to go out and see if I can get one more."

Henri nodded. "I think that's very wise. I know it seems like I'm crazy, but I want us to be ready for winter."

"No, I understand. I've spent so long thinking that I just needed to have shelter for winter, but you're right. We need food."

He took his rifle and went out for what she was certain would be the last time that day. They were fortunate enough that they lived in a valley where the game was plentiful. If Roy was willing to hunt for another few weeks and could keep bringing in as much meat as he was, they would be set for winter, and his parents would as well. And quite possibly her family, but she wasn't as worried about them. Bastian was an excellent hunter, as was Sam. It would all work out.

She put the roast into the water with the vegetables and hung the pot in the fireplace. Then she went out and cut a much larger roast and put it on a platter, carrying it to his parents' house.

Emma came to the door at her knock, and she eyed the bloody piece of meat. "That looks disgusting," she said.

"It does. But it will make a wonderful supper."

Mrs. Williams walked over and smiled at Henri. "I heard you were getting married today. And you're bringing me a present? I don't think it's supposed to work that way!"

Henri laughed. "Roy has already gotten two large elk today. I'm making elk roast for supper and thought you might enjoy the fresh meat as well. You'll be getting more of course, but the blood is still draining."

Mrs. Williams took the platter with the meat on it and took it into her kitchen, dumping it in a huge pot and hanging it over the fireplace. Henri was surprised she never once touched the meat. How odd.

Henri bit her lip, but she couldn't keep herself from asking, "Aren't you going to put water in with it? It'll dry out terribly without."

Mrs. Williams shook her head. "No, this is how I've always cooked meat."

Henri was glad she wasn't eating with his family that night. His mother really was a terrible cook. She didn't even seem to know the basics. "Well, I should get back to our cabin. I'm baking bread to go with our elk roast tonight."

"Wonderful!" Mrs. Williams smiled. "Have a wonderful supper. And best wishes."

Henri smiled. She'd worked so hard all day that she'd almost forgotten it was her wedding day. "Thank you!"

As she walked back toward the cabin, she wondered if she should offer to give Mrs. Williams cooking lessons. Even though the woman was a great deal older than she was, she didn't seem to have a clue how to make a good meal.

She hurried back into the cabin, and put an iron skillet onto the fire with the first loaf of bread in it. All the bread should be done for the day, and she wanted to kick herself for not thinking of baking it earlier. The wedding had just flung all reason from her mind.

When Roy came home an hour later, he was empty handed. "I didn't see anything else."

"That's fine. We probably have five-hundred pounds of meat out there. I know it's not enough for your family and us, but I don't think it will be much longer before we feel like we're completely ready for the winter."

She took the skillet out of the fire and dumped the bread out onto a towel on the table. Then she added the next loaf of bread to the fire. It should be done around the time supper was.

"Do you want to take this loaf of bread to your ma? I didn't smell any bread baking when I took them a roast earlier."

"I think that's a great idea. How should I carry it?"

She took a clean towel and wrapped the bread in it, showing him just where to hold it to keep it clean and not burn his hand. "That should work!"

He kissed her quickly. "Do you have more work to do after supper?" He was certainly hoping he wouldn't have to wait until late for his wedding night.

"Just the dishes. Tomorrow will be busy with the meat, though. I think you'll have to butcher all day, and I'll dry some for the winter." Henri laughed, shaking her head. "I feel like our entire lives are consumed with getting ready for the winter."

"I do too!" he said. "But, if we don't want to starve this winter, or freeze to death, we need to keep working. I was a little disappointed earlier that you wanted me to hunt all day and not spend time with you, but I realize now that you're right. We need to keep on our toes and keep doing as much as we can to make it through."

She grinned at him. "We'll have plenty of time to spend together this winter, when it's too cold to go out. Thanks for working toward winter with me. I'm really excited about all the game you got today. We're going to be set for winter with a few more elk. But we must clean these first."

"I'll be right back," he said, picking up the loaf of bread for his family. His ma never baked bread. He didn't think she liked it, but he knew the rest of the family would be pleased with the offering.

While Roy was gone, Henri set the table and served them each a plate, cutting up the bread and putting out a ball of butter. She would soon have to start churning butter again. That was one thing that had been so much easier on the trail. They'd just hung the cream under the wagons in the morning, and by noon, they had butter. Now she'd have to work for butter again. She hoped she could talk Roy into building her a butter churn.

When Roy came back, he had a big grin on his face. "I thought my pa was going to kiss me when I walked into their cabin with bread. Ma said she'd made it early in their marriage, but she always burned it, and Pa had asked her to stop making it."

"Do you think your ma would like me to teach her how to cook?" she asked. "I'd be happy to do it."

"Probably not a good idea," Roy said. "She's always been self-conscious about her cooking. I don't think I realized just how bad it was until recently. It was all I'd ever had."

"I understand. If you ever think she'd be open to it, I'd happily teach her a few things. She put the roast on the fire with no water. It's going to be hard and will be lacking flavor. I suggested water, and she told me she always made roast that way."

He washed his hands and sat down at the table, looking at his plate. "Is this how a roast is supposed to look?" he asked. He'd never seen one look so moist.

"That's how my ma always made them."

After their prayer, he took a small bite of the roast dipping it in the gravy on his mashed potatoes. He chewed slowly, finally giving her the verdict. "This is amazing!"

She smiled. "I love to cook. We have enough for our noon meal tomorrow."

"I'd gladly eat this repeatedly." He forked up another bite and swallowed it quickly.

"That's what you said about lunch!"

"I think I'm just going to say that I will happily eat anything you make."

She reached for the bread and buttered two pieces, handing him one. "Do you think you could make me a butter churn? This is my last ball of butter, and I can't make it by hanging a pail under the wagon anymore."

He nodded slowly. "Do you cook with a lot of butter?" he asked.

"Yes, of course. And I always want it for my bread."

He took a bite and sighed. "This is heavenly."

"I love baking bread. I almost forgot to bake today, and I'm sorry for that. I'll be putting bread into the oven throughout the evening. I plan to take several loaves of bread to my pa and brothers every couple of days. They're used to having fresh bread with every meal."

"And will you make their butter?" he asked.

"I will. Any way I can keep them fed will make me happy."

"All your brothers need to marry, so their wives can help you with the cooking."

"I really don't mind. My ma taught me there was joy in caring for others."

He smiled. "I think that sounds lovely. You are welcome to do whatever you want."

"Good. I really worried for a little while that you would feel neglected if I did things for my family."

"Not at all. I want you to do things that will keep them happy. Why wouldn't I? They're my family now too."

Henri smiled. "I thought you might be jealous of the time that I spent doing for them and not doing for you."

He chuckled. "Not at all. In the dead of winter, I may ask them to come to us for the bread, so you didn't have to carry it up the hill in the cold, but other than that, it's just fine."

She got up and removed the skillet from the fire, dropping the bread on a cloth, and adding the next loaf.

"How long will it take you to finish baking tonight?" he asked. He was already wishing he could drag her off to bed.

"Oh, no more than two hours. Usually, I bake in the mornings and have the bread ready in the afternoon. I just didn't think to start my baking today."

"Our morning was quite busy," he said grinning at her as he took her hand in his.

"That, and I'd baked bread when I got up this morning for my pa and brothers. How was I supposed to remember to bake twice?"

"Do you bake fresh bread every day?" he asked.

"Most days I do. I make extra on Saturdays, so I don't have to do any baking on Sundays. I do cook on Sundays though. I hate that I must break the Sabbath to keep my family from being hungry."

"Oh, I wouldn't worry about that," he said. "God knows that we all need to eat every day, which includes Sundays."

She ate her last bite and watched as he ate every drop of food on his plate, and then mopped up the last of the gravy with bread. "Do you want more?" she asked. "There's plenty."

He shook his head. "No, that's fine. I'm full, and I'll be looking forward to eating this again tomorrow."

"What all do you have planned for tomorrow?" she asked.

"Splitting more wood and dealing with the elks. We need to split up meat between my family and us. Maybe take some to your family if you want."

"If you'll get me another large roast in the morning, I'll make it for my family, and we'll take them a few roasts. They're all good hunters, but they're not so great at cooking."

"Few men are," he said.

After she'd finished the bread and washed all the dishes, she sat down at the table with him. The only furniture in the house was the bed, table, and benches, so she really didn't have a lot of options. She wanted a bath badly, but she'd have to bring water in and boil it to make it happen, and they didn't have enough water to do it. He had a rain barrel out to collect water, though. It was funny how much they now relied on rainwater.

"I think I'm done for the night," she said. "Do you have chickens?"

He nodded. "Well, my parents do, and they have plenty for all of us to have eggs every morning. Ma does well with her chickens. They were mostly in their cages the whole way here, but sometimes she'd let them out for the morning walk, and they actually followed her along the trail. I have no idea how she did that."

"That's fun! I do well with cows, but not so much with chickens. I'll have to get her to teach me her tricks."

He smiled. "Emma is just as good with chickens as Ma is."

"How's her cooking?" she asked.

"About like Ma's."

Henri knew Jared wouldn't be pleased with that, but she didn't want to interfere. Obviously, his family had lived just fine with his mother's cooking. She wasn't sure quite how, but they had.

"If you're finished with all your work for the night, perhaps we should get ready for bed." Roy had been waiting for their wedding night since the first moment he saw her in Independence.

She nodded. "Can you give me ten minutes to get ready?" she asked.

He frowned. "What do you want me to do during that time?"

"Oh, go milk a cow or split some more wood."

"It would be easier if I stayed inside and helped you undress."

Her cheeks turned beet red. "Please?"

Roy got up and went outside, but it was obvious to her he was reluctant to do so. She heard him using the axe, though, so she jumped up and undressed, putting on her nightgown. She was glad no one was outside because she hadn't made curtains yet, and the window was open. She was pretty sure she had enough fabric to do so, and she'd start on them after the elk were readied for winter.

In her nightgown, Henri climbed beneath the sheets on the bed. It was a strange feeling to know Roy would be in at any time to consummate her marriage. She wanted to tell him she wasn't ready, but she also wanted babies. She wasn't sure which she wanted more...to wait or to have babies.

When Roy came in a few moments later, he turned down the lanterns throughout the small cabin. There were only four, but they made the cabin very bright because the room was so small.

After the lights were out, Henri could hear him undressing. When he slid into bed beside her, and pulled her toward him, she was surprised to discover he was wearing no clothes. "Aren't you supposed to wear a nightshirt?" she asked.

He chuckled. "There's nothing we're supposed to do. Except consummate our marriage."

"I'm very nervous about that!"

"To tell the truth, I am too. I've never done this before either, but...I'm nervous and eager both. I've been looking forward to this night since I first saw you in Independence."

She closed her eyes for a moment. She'd been imagining his babies all that time, but she'd never once thought about how they'd make them together. Thankfully, her mother had explained to her how babies were made, and she was aware of what would happen.

"I want to make you happy," Henri finally said.

He smiled. "I want to make you happy as well." He pressed his lips to hers and kissed her more passionately than he had before. His hands roamed over her body on top of her nightgown.

He caught her nipple between one thumb and forefinger, and slowly teased it with his fingers. "I don't think you're supposed to touch me there!" Henri said. Her mother hadn't talked about men touching a woman's breast.

"It's fine. We're married. I can touch you all over."

She nodded. He'd talked to someone other than her mother about this night.

She decided that she wouldn't worry about what he was doing anymore, and she wrapped her arms around him and enjoyed his touch. When he finally moved to cover her and make them one, she was eager for him.

A short while later, he lay on his back, gasping for breath, while she snuggled right into him. Sometime during their time of passion, he'd thrown her nightgown onto the floor. "I should get my nightgown."

"No. I like to touch your skin."

So, she decided she could sleep without her nightgown, though she'd never even considered doing so before. Even on their hottest days on the trail.

She was growing sleepy and yawned widely. "I think I need sleep. It's been a busy day."

"It has." He turned her chin up so he could kiss her once more, and then closed his own eyes. "Tomorrow we'll work hard."

"We'll work hard every day," she responded before closing her eyes.

He smiled at how pretty she looked by the light of the moon shining in the window. He hoped she never got around to making curtains for that one window. He liked to be able to see her in the night.

Chapter Eight

Henri woke before dawn the next morning, as she always did. She climbed out of bed, dressed quickly, and put a log on the fire. She was surprised at how chilly it was. It got colder in Clover Creek more quickly than it had in Indiana.

She wanted to make eggs for their breakfast, but they would have to wait until he was awake and ready to go get the eggs. She put the coffee pot on the stove and then found the fabric she'd brought for curtains. Henri and her ma had both chosen fabric for curtains for their new homes. It was the one indulgence her pa had agreed to.

She sat quietly at the table with only one lantern on, and she stitched the curtains. When Roy finally woke as the sun was rising, he rubbed his eyes wearily. "What are you doing?"

"I'm making curtains for our window. At night, I feel like I'm being watched by everyone, even though, I know it's not true."

"All right." He was without shame as he stood and got into his work clothes. "I'll go and get eggs. Six enough?"

She nodded. "Do you prefer your eggs fried or scrambled?"

"I've only ever had scrambled."

"Would you like scrambled this morning, or would you prefer I made them how I like them?"

"You have yet to feed me something I don't love. Just make them how you like them."

Henri smiled. "I will then."

She toasted six pieces of toast, buttering each as soon as it was done. Then she heated up her iron skillet, putting butter in the bottom of it. Usually, she would make bacon and fry the eggs in the grease, but she didn't want to go through their bacon stores before she knew how much meat they'd have for the winter.

Roy came back into the house with six eggs in a basket. "Ma said we could have six eggs every morning if we wanted to."

"That would be wonderful. Then on mornings I don't make eggs, I'll be able to make a cake. Eggs make all the difference in the world when you're baking."

"And you'd frost the cake?" he asked, his eyes wide. He'd had few cakes growing up, mostly when he visited others.

"Of course." She cracked each egg into the skillet before returning it to the fireplace. She dreamed of the day she'd have a stove to cook on. Flipping them when the eggs were mostly finished cooking, she saw him watching everything she did intensely. "Do you want to learn to cook?"

"Not right now. I'm just interested in how you do things so differently than my ma."

She put four eggs on a plate for him, and two on a plate for her. Then she added the four slices of toast for him and two for herself. She put the plates on the table and got coffee for both of them.

When she sat down, they prayed, and then he eyed the eggs. "How do I eat them?" he asked.

She showed him how to break the yolk and dip the toast into the runny yolk. "This doesn't taste anything like eggs," he said, trying her way. "But it's good!"

"It's just a different way of making them. I make scrambled too, but I tend to prefer these. If you want scrambled, I can make them another day." She could only imagine what the eggs his mother made had tasted like.

"I could eat them this way every day!"

"I'll do some scrambled as well so you can compare. Maybe I'll make scrambled tomorrow."

"Or you could make a cake tomorrow. I'm good with either one."

She smiled. "Why don't I do pancakes for breakfast in the morning, and I'll make a cake for dessert as well. They both need eggs, but just four would be enough for all that."

"I almost feel guilty loving your cooking as much as I do. I feel like I'm being disloyal to Ma."

"I won't tell her if you don't."

He grinned. "That's easy to agree to." He finished eating and pushed his plate away. "I'm going to go split wood for an hour or so, and then I'll start butchering the elk. The elk are going to take most of the day."

"Sounds good to me. I'll dry some and salt some. Should I do the same for your family's meat, or will your ma prefer to do theirs herself."

"She prides herself on her jerky, so I would let her do it. I haven't tasted your jerky."

"Your ma's really is good. That's what I used for our lunch yesterday."

"All right." He stood. "I'm going to get that wood chopped."

She did the breakfast dishes while he chopped wood. After making the bed and sweeping, she felt that she was ready for a day of preserving meat.

She walked outside to find a huge stack of logs against the house, and Roy slicing up the meat. With as cold as it was at night, there was no danger of the meat having gone bad.

"How can I help?"

"I need you to do the drying and salting. Nothing else."

Henri nodded. "Should I come out to get the meat, or will you bring it to me?"

"I'll bring it in."

"Would you mind cutting off a big roast for my pa and brothers? Then I can take it to them when I take the bread."

"Oh, sure." He cut off a large hunk of meat. "I'll carry it in. I know how women are about raw meat."

Henri cocked her head to one side. "And how are we?"

"I've never met a woman who was willing to touch raw meat."

"How can we cook if we don't touch raw meat?" His assumption made no sense to her. Of course, she'd seen his mother avoid touching meat just yesterday.

"You don't mind?"

She shook her head. "My ma taught me that's the only way to cook, so I've been doing it since I was a little girl." She held her hands out, and he put the meat in them, watching her as if he expected her to drop it. "Thank you."

She carried the meat inside and made the same basic meal she and Roy had eaten the night before. Roast, onion, carrots, and potatoes. While that cooked, she started her bread for the day. It seemed to her she should be baking enough for his family, her family, and her own. She'd continue to bake ten loaves and split them between them. Each of their families could have four loaves per day, and she and Roy would keep two.

Roy brought in several large hunks of meat. "Are these for us or for your family?" she asked. "That's too much for us for even two meals. I think it would be a better amount for your family."

"All right," he said, putting the board he'd been balancing the meat on onto the table. "I'll go tell Pa that he can come get it anytime he wants to."

"All right. I could cut these in half to be the right size for us if you'd prefer."

He nodded. "Let's do that. I'd rather get ours done, and then have Ma come get hers."

"As soon as the roast for my family finishes cooking, I'll start a brine to preserve the meat."

"All right. Let me get back to chopping meat."

As soon as the roast was done for her family, she pulled out her second cook pot, thankful that there were two for her to work with. In that pot, she put water, and salt, putting it over the fire to bring to a boil.

Then she picked up the other pot, as well as a kitchen towel with bread wrapped in it, and she walked outside, stopping to let Roy know she was going up the hill.

"Do you want me to carry that?" he asked. "It looks heavy."

She smiled. "It's not bad. I'll be back in thirty minutes or so."

Heading up the hill, she ran into Jared, who had just come from the Williams' cabin. "I'm carrying this up to the cabin for your supper tonight."

"Emma offered to come up and cook for us."

Biting her lip, Henri didn't say anything about the other woman's cooking ability. "Maybe you should take this just in case," she said.

He looked at her with narrowed eyes but took the big pot from her.

"I have bread too. Lots and lots of bread."

"Good. I don't know if I could get through a day without eating your delicious bread," he said.

"I'm trying to be sure you don't have to. Until you marry that is."

"If she's a terrible cook, I'm sending her to you for cooking lessons. And I'll expect bread every day."

Henri smiled sweetly. "That sounds like it could be fun. She's already my sister-in-law, but soon she'll be my sister-in-law twice over. It'll be fun to teach her."

"You sound like you already know she's a terrible cook."

"I've never eaten her cooking," Henri said honestly. She hadn't eaten Mrs. Williams's cooking either, though she knew how terrible she was by comments Roy had made.

"Oh, then you have no idea."

"No." They reached the cabin, and Henri went inside, getting a towel from the kitchen and wrapping the bread in it. She took out the big pot her pa had, and she dumped the cooked roast, onion, potatoes, and carrots into it. "There. Now you have backup or food for tomorrow. Whatever you need."

"Thanks, I think."

"If you want to cook for all of you then just tell me. I won't bring any more food up."

"I know we're at least going to need bread every day," he said.

She laughed, taking her pot back and tucking the cloth into the pocket of her apron. "Goodbye, big brother."

"How do you like being married?" he asked as she turned away.

"It's certainly different, but it's good. I think I'm going to be very happy with Roy."

"Good. Go home."

She laughed. "I'm trying to, but you keep talking to me!"

He chuckled but said nothing else, and she left.

When she arrived at the cabin, she saw his father was there to help with the butchering, so she went straight inside. Henri took the boiling brine off the stove, and immediately stuck one of the pans of bread into the fire.

Then she cut the roasts in half. Then she took jars that were in the corner with the other supplies. She poured brine into each one and added one piece of meat to each before she screwed the lid onto the jar. There would be enough roasts to have one per week all winter, and that would feed them two meals each time. Perfect.

He brought in some hunks of meat that were too small to be roasts, and she planned to dry them all. The jerky made could then feed them with meals like the one she'd cooked for lunch the previous day.

After sealing the brine with the meat, she took the bread off the stove, and then put the food that was left from their supper the night before on the fire and heated it up. As soon as she took it off the fireplace, she added another pan of bread. She would send two home with Mr. Williams if he wanted them.

She set the table, and then called Roy for lunch. Mr. Williams was still there, so she offered him lunch as well. There was enough food for three of them.

"I'd love to," Mr. Williams said.

She set another place at the table and poured coffee for the three of them. When the two men had washed their hands, they sat at the table, and Mr. Williams said their prayer, praising God for all he had brought their family through.

Mr. Williams took his first bite of the roast and closed his eyes with pleasure. "This is how my ma always made her roasts. It's delicious."

Henri smiled. "My ma taught me to make them this way."

"This isn't the same meat you gave us for supper last night, is it?"

Henri was afraid to answer. She didn't want him to think her cooking was better than his wife's.

"Yes, it's the same," Roy said, when he realized, she wasn't going to answer Pa's question.

"Then why was our meat all dried out last night?"

Henri ducked her head. She knew the answer, but she didn't want to insult his wife.

"Henri," Mr. Williams said, "do you know what my wife is doing wrong when she makes roast?"

"She's not adding water, or vegetables. The vegetables season it and the water keeps the meat moist." Henri mumbled.

When Mr. Williams took a second piece of her bread, he sighed happily. "We are very grateful for the bread you made. We'd all been wanting bread for a long time, but I'm afraid my wife isn't much of a baker."

"I'm still making bread for my family as well," she said. "I wouldn't mind bringing you some every day. If you gave me some flour to use, of course. We won't have enough for the winter if I kept making bread for three families."

"Of course. I'll bring you a fifty-pound bag of flour after we finish eating."

"That would be fine." Henri was careful not to look at Roy. She knew he didn't think she should be talking about his mother's cooking, but what else could she do?

"Is there more?" Mr. Williams asked, surprising her.

"Yes, there's enough for both of you to have another plate," Henri said. "Would you like more as well, Roy?"

"I would very much appreciate more," Roy said, but he didn't look at her. That's when she knew he was angry. But what could she do?

She filled both plates and refilled their coffee. Then sat down and finished her own meal. "I think I'm drying everything else. We have enough to have two meals from roasts all winter long. That should be enough, and I know you'll keep hunting game throughout the winter."

"Are you still fine with doing all the work with the cattle this winter, while I bring in game for all of us?" Roy asked his father.

"Of course," Mr. Williams said. "Just so all the work gets done, I think we can divide it any way we like. And we both know you're much better with a rifle than I am."

Roy nodded. "Then that will be the plan."

"Roy told me he invited your family to supper on Saturday night. What do you like to eat?" Henri asked.

Mr. Williams shrugged. "I'd eat this every day all winter, honestly. But I'd be happy with whatever you enjoy cooking."

"All right. We'll figure it out then." She thought perhaps she could make some jerky gravy and rice for them, because it was a very inexpensive meal, but she'd talk to Roy about it later. He would have a better idea of what his family ate. She could also make some venison pies, but he'd have to get some venison. She wondered how her venison pie would taste with elk instead. She had a feeling it would be just as good. Perhaps she'd make that.

Roy shook his head at her. "Are you woolgathering?"

Henri smiled. "I was thinking about different things I could cook when your family comes to supper."

"Make sure there's bread," Mr. Williams said. "I can't believe you can make such delicious bread in a fireplace."

"I worked hard on perfecting the bread while we were on the trail. My pa and brothers complained at first, because it wasn't as good. But Ma and I worked at it, and we figured it out."

"Was your ma as good of a cook as you are?" Mr. Williams asked.

"She taught me everything I know," Henri said modestly. She knew she'd been a better cook than her ma, but it wasn't by much. Ma had still made a few things better than Henri did.

Mr. Williams patted his stomach. "I believe I'll take the already butchered meat back to the cabin. Then I'll come and help you some more." He looked at Henri. "That was the most delicious meal I've eaten in a long time. Thanks for inviting me."

After his pa left, Roy looked at Henri. "You couldn't leave well enough alone, could you?"

"I tried…"

He shook his head. "I don't want you making my ma look bad, just because you're a better cook. Not many women could hold a candle to your meals."

"Would you like me to deliberately burn supper when your family comes?" she asked. It would take everything inside her to do it, but she knew she could.

He shook his head. "No. While I don't want my ma to know how much better you are than her, I also want to show off your wonderful cooking. I know it makes no sense. I just don't want Ma's feelings hurt."

"I'll try not to hurt them," she said. "I'm sorry if you feel I said too much to your pa."

"I don't. I just…I don't even know what to say. I just don't like Ma to feel badly."

Henri got up and cleared the table, then took another loaf of bread from the oven. "Is it all right if I take them a couple loaves of bread?"

For a moment, Roy looked torn but then he nodded. "Just because I'm worried about my ma, doesn't mean they should have to eat her cooking."

"Emma is going to cook for my family tonight," she said softly.

He groaned. "She's not going to be able to hide what a terrible cook she is. She's even worse than ma. She tries, but she hasn't been shown how to do anything."

"Jared told me if she couldn't cook, he was going to make her come to me for cooking lessons. I hope it doesn't come to that, but it sounds like he's marrying her no matter what kind of cook she is."

"I guess that's good." Roy shook his head. "There's no way she's going to measure up to what your family expects from meals."

"There's a back up meal for them if they're unhappy with her cooking. It shouldn't be a big deal. My family knows not to embarrass her over it. They'll eat anything like a bunch of goats. They just won't be happy about it."

He chuckled. "I like how you compare the men in your family to goats. May I quote you on that?"

"Never."

Henri finished up the dishes and started to work slicing the meat up thinner to make it dry faster. She really would prefer to use a salt brine on it all, but she'd run out of jars. Jerky would have to do.

Chapter Nine

When they joined Roy's family for supper on Friday night, Henri took a cake and several loaves of bread. Then if she couldn't eat the meal prepared, she could at least make it look like she was eating.

Roy carried the cake, while she carried the bread. One loaf was still warm from the fireplace. Roy opened the door without knocking, which felt a little off to Henri, until she realized she did the same with her father's cabin.

She hadn't cooked a full meal for her family since she'd made the roast, and Jared told her Emma was cooking for them. She didn't ask, and she really didn't want to know, how well Emma did at cooking supper.

They were greeted by his family, but his mother was rigid, as if she didn't want them there. "I made a roast," Mrs. Williams said, but she said it in a way that made Henri feel like she'd done something wrong.

"From the elk?" Henri asked. "Those have been the best roasts! I just wish I had more jars to preserve the meat."

Mrs. Williams gave her a long hard look. "I have two dozen more. I'm not going to be preserving the meat with salt this year. You are welcome to them."

"Are you certain?" Henri asked. The idea of being able to do some venison roasts and more elk roasts excited her.

"Yes, of course. I do better with my jerky."

As they all gathered around the table, Henri peeked at the roast and saw it had been done correctly. You could see how moist the roast was.

After the prayer, they passed the food in a circle around the table. "Everything looks delicious, Mrs. Williams."

Mrs. Williams grunted.

As soon as Henri's plate was filled, she took a bite of the roast. "This is delicious." She was exaggerating a bit. The roast had been cooked alone with absolutely no seasoning, but at least she could bite into it.

Mr. Williams nodded. "This is the best roast you've ever made."

"If I use your jars, I'll make sure that I get you some of the roasts," Henri said with a smile.

Mrs. Williams still looked annoyed, but she said, "I'll trade some jerky for the roasts."

"That would be wonderful!" Henri said enthusiastically. "I find your jerky to be some of the best I've ever eaten!" Except her own of course, but she wasn't about to say that aloud.

"That sounds like it's a fair trade," Roy said, worried that things would be tense between him and his family over the way things were cooked, which he found silly.

Mr. Williams eyed the cake they'd brought. "We are going to have cake, aren't we?"

"For dessert," Henri said. "This cake is a bit of an experiment. I baked some dried cherries into the cake, and then I added some water to a few more dried cherries, and I cut them into tiny pieces, which I mixed in with the frosting. I'm not sure how it turned out, so I'll need to hear from everyone what you think of it."

"You didn't have to bring anything, Henrietta," Mrs. Williams said. "You were only asked to come."

Mr. Williams frowned. "But we're very grateful for the bread and the cake," he said. "Aren't we, Ma?"

"Of course," Mrs. Williams looked down at her food.

Henri looked over at Emma to ask how she was doing, but Emma's eyes were red rimmed with tears. She decided to not ask anything that may upset the other girl. She was afraid she already knew what was wrong.

It was hard making conversation with as upset as Mrs. Williams and Emma were. Henri finally stopped trying, giving her attention to the burned rice and unseasoned meat on her plate. She could eat the meat with no real trouble, but the rice was very hard to choke down. Now she understood why Roy had said he hated rice.

As soon as they were all finished eating, Mr. Williams walked to get the cake off the bed he shared with his wife. They'd brought the empty mattresses from home but had added dried grass when they arrived. The beds were comfortable, but they hadn't had to bring full mattresses, which would have weighed down the wagons.

Mr. Williams set the cake in the middle of the table. He got a knife and cut it into eight pieces, though there were seven people to eat it. "I do believe I'm saving an extra piece for myself. This looks and smells amazing," he said.

Everyone was served a piece of the cake, and Henri was nervous as she took her first bite, but she'd always had a knack for combining foods she'd never eaten together.

After taking her first bite she smiled. The cake was delicious.

Emma hadn't said a word since Henri and Roy had arrived, but she said, "Will you teach me to bake cakes like this? And bread?"

"Of course, I will," Henri said. "We'll pick a day, and you can come over and learn to make those two things."

"Thank you," Emma said, going back to eating her cake, but not looking any happier than she had a while before.

Mrs. Williams glared at Henri then, and Henri wanted to apologize, but she didn't know how. *What could she say? I'm sorry I can cook, and you can't...Or even better, I'm going to teach your whole family to cook, so they can stop eating meals that are half burnt with no seasoning?* She decided it was best to keep her mouth shut, and so she did.

Roy seemed to understand Henri's discomfort. "I've got enough firewood chopped up that I'm going to take tomorrow to hunt again. What other game should I try for?" he asked.

Henri decided to offer her suggestions once they were home, but Mr. Williams had a couple of things to ask for. "I'd love a turkey," he said. "Turkey dinners are one of my favorite meals, if they're made with dressing. Especially with sausage and onions."

Henri smiled. "Do you prefer your dressing to be bread or cornbread?"

"I've never had cornbread. My ma always made a wonderful bread stuffing that I ate more than my share of."

"If Roy gets a turkey, I'll make both kinds of stuffing for the meals with turkey. What else do you like to have with turkey?"

"Oh, so many things. Mashed potatoes and gravy. Caramelized carrots. Lots of fresh bread. Pies. Umm...Oh, I almost forgot baked squash, and did I mention pies?"

Henri smiled. "I'll do my best to make those things happen."

"That would please me. I haven't had a decent turkey dinner since my ma passed away, about five years after we married, wasn't it, Ma?"

Mrs. Williams nodded. "That's a lot of cooking for just one person."

"Well, since Emma has expressed a desire to learn to cook new things, I think I'll have her help me with the cooking. I know I can do apple and cherry pies with dried fruit, which both sound delicious. We'll top them with whipped cream!"

"What can I make for the meal?" Mrs. Williams asked.

"Anything you want to make," Henri said. "If it's all right with you, we'll invite my family as well, and have a huge meal for all of us."

"How often did you help your mother cook?" Mr. Williams asked.

"Every day. I've loved to cook since I was a little girl and my ma taught me to make my first pie. I'm very thankful I knew how to cook after my ma died." Henri bit her lip for a moment. "My brothers still wanted their favorite meals, but it was up to me to make them."

"No wonder you are such a good cook," Mr. Williams said. "You've practiced your whole life."

Henri nodded. "I've never really enjoyed cleaning or sewing, but I love to cook and bake."

"You can sure tell by how good your pies and bread are. And that roast you served this week was the most wonderful thing I've put in my mouth for years."

"Thank you, sir," Henri knew the subject needed to change to avoid unnecessary hurt for Roy's mother and sisters, but she wasn't sure how to make Mr. Williams stop.

Roy piped up, instead of leaving it all up to Henri. "I'll try for more elk, some venison, and turkey then. And then I'll chop some more wood. Do you have enough wood for winter, Pa?"

Mr. Williams shrugged. "I don't think I do. But I'll get back to it as soon as I can."

"That sounds like a good idea," Mrs. Williams said. "We're going to need to keep warm and fed all winter, and both require firewood."

"When I feel like we're set for winter food-wise, I'd love to help you with the wood, Pa," Roy said. "I think we're set wood wise, but it would be nice if neither of us had to go out for more trees in the middle of winter."

"I agree," Mr. Williams said. "Yes, if you have a little time, I'd love the help. If not, I'll just keep chopping."

When they left that night, Roy looked over at Henri. "My family has already figured out that the way you cook is better than Ma's. And Ma's feelings are hurt. Pa made her put water on the roast, but it still wasn't nearly as good as yours. I'm just not sure if the two of you are ever going to be able to be close."

"I hope we'll get past this," Henri said, frowning. "I feel pretty sure Jared told Emma she needs to take cooking lessons from me. That's probably why she looks so sad all the time."

"Our families are very different, but I didn't see that at first. We'll find a way to see eye-to-eye though. Pa sure likes the way you do things better than the way we always have." He shook his head. "And we're having my family over tomorrow, right?"

"We are. I really like the idea of cooking a full meal for them. Do you have any idea what they'd prefer? I'm thinking jerky gravy over rice with a side of green beans. Or I could do a pot pie. Or I bet I could get my hands on a couple of pullets, and we could have chicken and dumplings? Or is there anything else you can think of?"

"I like the idea of pot pie. But you'll have to make a few."

"Oh, of course. When Ma and I made them for my family, we'd make one for Ma and me to share, and then one each for the men."

He chuckled. "Same principle would work with us. One each for my pa and I, and then one for every two females."

"That would leave me with an extra half-pie for lunch on Sunday. You know what? I'll make two extra pies. They're easy to reheat for the next day."

He smiled. "Sounds good to me. What meat will you use?"

She shrugged. "What are you going to bring me tomorrow?"

He sighed. "I have no idea!"

"Well, I could do turkey if tomorrow is the day, you get a turkey. I could use venison, or elk even. Just get me some meat, and I'll make it work. I think bear meat would even be good in my pot pies."

"I'll see what I can do. And you'll use some of the elk we already have if I can't get something tomorrow?"

"Sure, I can do that." She sighed. "I'm sorry I've hurt your mother's feelings. I never would have done that deliberately."

"I know. It'll all work out." He wasn't so sure though. Perhaps it had been a mistake not getting to know her better before marrying her. He certainly didn't need a wife who was always upsetting his mother. But he'd been in love with Henri, and no one else.

"I'm glad everyone liked the cake tonight. I'll do a more traditional cake for tomorrow," she said.

"That'll work." When they arrived back at their own cabin, he opened the door for her. His little wife was so much more than he'd realized when he was courting her.

"Would you mind if we did pancakes or johnny cakes for breakfast in the morning? I'd like to save eggs for the cake."

"That's fine. I love everything you cook." But there was more to life than cooking all the time. He wasn't sure why she didn't see that. "We forgot to get the jars from Ma. Is it okay if I run back for them?"

"Of course!" she said. "Do you want me to come with you?"

Roy shook his head. "No thanks. You should wash that empty cake plate. Everyone obviously loved it."

"I will."

He left, going back toward his parents' house, and he had no idea what to say to make things better.

When he arrived, his parents were arguing, and he'd rarely heard them argue. He waited before he opened the door, listening to make sure the argument wasn't about Henri.

"I don't understand why you're being so stubborn about this!" Pa said. "You always told me you wished you were a better cook. We have a new daughter-in-law that can cook just about anything. Why aren't you taking advantage of her knowledge and learning from her?"

"Because she's a child! No one in this family has complained about my cooking. What could she possibly teach me?" Ma responded.

"I'm certainly happy our oldest daughter is more sensible than you are. Maybe I'll send all three girls, and she can teach them to cook. Then we could have some decent meals around here!"

Roy stood at the door with his eyes closed for a moment. They were fighting about Henri. He couldn't understand why, but they were. After a moment, he opened the door, pretending he'd heard nothing. "Henri asked me to come back for the jars you said you had."

Instead of continuing to fight with her husband, Ma turned away and went into the cellar for jars. His father looked at him across the room. "Your mother is a stubborn woman."

"I'm sorry, Pa."

"You've done nothing wrong."

Emma walked over to Roy, looking embarrassed. "Is it all right if Henri teaches me to cook? I was ashamed of how badly supper turned out when I cooked for the Applebys."

"Of course, it's all right. Henri is the best person to learn from. She can make anything. I didn't know food could taste as good as she makes it!" Roy felt bad that she was embarrassed, but he was happy she was willing to learn. There was no reason, she couldn't someday cook as well as Henri.

"Thank you. I may go over in the morning, and just spend the day learning from her."

"I'll let her know to expect you. If you come early enough, she'll show you how to make pancakes."

Emma looked confused. "I already know how to make pancakes."

"You know how to make pancakes with eggshells in them that are burnt on at least one side every time. Let Henri teach you to do it without shells or burning." Roy now knew what her beau was used to eating, and he knew Jared would never put up with eating her cooking until she'd improved a great deal.

"All right." Emma had tears in her eyes again. "I wish it wasn't so important to him."

"It wasn't important to me until I realized there were better ways." He shook his head. "I just hate that you and Ma feel so bad about it."

"It doesn't matter. I'm going to be a better cook if it's the last thing I do!"

He chuckled. "I appreciate the enthusiasm, but there's no need to kill yourself to be a better cook."

"I guess not."

Ma came up the stairs then, carrying another two dozen jars. She gave them all to Roy. "Good thing I didn't slip on those stairs," she said. "Wouldn't that have made your little Henri happy?"

Roy's face hardened. "Henri is happy, and she's hoping to be close to you. I wish you could see that she's just trying to help."

Emma opened the door for him, and he walked back toward the cabin he shared with his wife. How had he been so blind? Henri was doing nothing wrong, and neither was his ma. But Pa was right. Ma was stubborn. He had to tell Henri she was doing a great job at everything. Who got mad at their new bride for being a wonderful cook? He'd obviously lost his mind trying to protect his mother.

As he walked home, he realized he'd been doing everything wrong where Henri was concerned. She wasn't prideful about her cooking, and she eagerly tried to help others. She was the best wife he could have asked for.

He kicked the door slightly when he got home, so Henri would open it for him. His hands were too full to open it himself.

He immediately put the jars onto the table. "That should be more than enough, shouldn't it?"

She nodded. "They're large jars. I can put up meat for us and both our families. Thank you for getting them for me." Henri stepped into Roy's arms and held him tight. "I'll work harder at being a better wife. I promise."

He rested his cheek on her head and thought about what he could do to make her realize that she was perfect as she was, and he loved her.

Chapter Ten

Emma was there before Roy was even awake the following morning. She'd brought their six eggs for the morning with her. When she realized Roy was asleep, she frowned. "Am I too early?"

Henri grinned. "When your brother wakes up, you're going to want to step outside for a minute while he dresses, but otherwise you're just fine. I'm always awake before sunup." Watching the sun rise was something Henri had always done with her mother, and doing it now, made her feel closer to her ma.

"That's so early!"

"My ma taught me it was the right way to be. It makes it easier to have food on the table when the menfolk wake up."

Emma sighed. "Your ma taught you very different things than my ma. She figured the men could wait to eat until she was awake."

Henri sighed. "My ma thought it was her duty to make her family as comfortable as she could. And she taught me to be the same. I don't want to cause more friction between you and your mother, but I'm so happy to teach you my little tips and tricks of cooking." Serving her family truly was an honor. She might not enjoy doing laundry, but she knew it made their days more pleasant.

"Let's do it then!"

Henri quickly demonstrated the right way to crack an egg, something she'd known since she was five. But she felt that she needed to start at the beginning with Emma.

Emma focused as she stirred the batter. "It's not crunching like it usually does. Is that okay?"

"Crunching? Oh, you were getting shells in the batter. We need to avoid shells, and if you realize you accidentally dumped some in the batter, you'll need to fish them out."

By the time Roy woke up, the pancakes were finished. They'd made twelve for the three of them. "Usually I do bacon with them, but I don't want to waste meat this close to winter."

"But you'll show me how to make bacon crisp and not burnt?" Emma asked.

"Of course, I will."

Roy looked over at his sister and wife working together and smiled. "Hey, Emma? You're going to have to go for a quick walk so I can get dressed."

"I will," Emma said, hurrying out the door.

"I'm glad you're teaching her to cook," Roy said. "No one should believe that the way they've been fed their entire lives is the right way when it's the disgusting way. I feel like I've put on a lot of weight since we started courting."

"It looks good on you," Henri said, smiling over her shoulder.

"Well, I'm glad you think so." He got out of bed and put on his work clothes. His morning would be filled with hunting, and he knew he'd be chilly. That was fine though if it helped them get ready for the winter.

"Emma made the pancakes this morning. I explained and demonstrated a few things, but she did the rest. Be gentle with your comments."

"I will. I'm proud of her for coming to you to learn."

"I am too."

There was a tentative knock on the door. "I'm dressed," Roy called, and the door opened.

"We have a little bit of butter left. I need to get a churn soon," Henri said.

Roy sighed. "I forgot to make your churn, but I've discovered I like to eat butter on everything, so I'll do that this afternoon if I get game this morning."

"That would be wonderful." Henri looked at Emma. "Would you like to learn to churn butter?"

Emma nodded. "Does Jared like butter?"

"On everything he can think to put it on. Maybe we'll all do it together. Your sisters could come as well. My arms are so sore by the end."

"Then we'll learn it too and help you."

Henri smiled. "Now sit down and eat. Try butter and syrup on your pancakes. It's delicious that way."

When all three were seated and the prayer had been said, Emma took her first bite of her pancakes, and her entire face lit up. "They're actually good!"

"They are. They're as good as mine. Jared loves pancakes, so you're going to be able to make them a lot without trouble." Henri was thrilled Emma had one breakfast down. If she could learn just a couple more, she would be set for a while.

"Oh, good!"

Roy bit into the pancakes and grinned at his sister. "You did it."

"We have no food left from last night, so we'll need to make lunch. How would you feel if we made rice with a jerky gravy over it? It's become another staple of what I cook," Henri said.

Emma grinned. "I'd love to learn to make that. I don't like rice much, but if your brother does, then I need to learn."

Roy shook his head. "You don't like rice when Ma makes it. I love Henri's rice."

"It shouldn't be crunchy, or burnt," Henri said.

"Well, that's the only way I've had it." Emma looked at Henri. "I want to like it."

"Trust me, you'll like it my way."

As soon as breakfast was over, Roy headed out to hunt, and the women did the dishes together. "Is it hard to make rice?" Emma asked.

"Not at all. I'll have you cooking a bunch of things by the end of the day. If you want to stay and learn that is." Henri didn't want to assume that she should take up the other girl's time with cooking lessons.

"I'll stay if you'll keep teaching."

"I will."

Roy was home an hour later with a deer. It wasn't nearly as large as the elk had been, but it was enough for the pot pies, and would be enough to save a bit of venison for the winter. "I'll let it bleed out while I work on your butter churn. Then after lunch, I'll bring you a chunk for supper."

"Perfect," Henri said, smiling. "Now, we're going to learn to bake bread."

"In a fireplace?" Emma asked, her eyes wide.

"That's how I make the bread I take to your house every day."

Emma squared her shoulders. "Teach me."

Henri quickly copied the receipt she had for bread and gave the new copy to Emma. "That's your receipt. I want you to follow along as we mix this." Henri explained each step before she even started the process.

Mixing up ten loaves of bread, as she'd been doing, Henri explained everything as she went. "Now, we have to knead it."

"I don't even know what that means!"

"You will in a minute."

The dough was rising while they made their lunch. Each step was explained by Henri in a way that made perfect sense to Emma.

"That's not how Ma cooks rice. Do you always use water?"

"Always."

"I think that's what Ma does wrong. She just puts it in the skillet and cooks it over the fire."

Henri had no idea what to say to that. "I've never seen anyone make rice that way." She went on to show Emma the right way to make gravy from jerky while the rice was cooking. "Now let's punch down the bread."

Emma followed Henri and imitated everything she did.

"We're going to form it into large balls, and once it's risen again, we'll make it in the skillet. I still prefer bread from an oven, but this is almost as good."

Once all the dough was at one end of the table, Henri cleaned the other half so lunch could be served.

When Roy came inside, he said, "That looks delicious. How much did you help, Emma?"

Emma smiled. "Henri told me what to do with each part of the process, and I followed instructions."

After their prayer, Roy took one bite of the mixture and nodded. "You learn quickly."

Emma practically glowed with the compliment.

By the time his family was there for supper, Emma had a small pile of receipts to use so she could cook on her own. When her ma walked in, Emma ran to her. "Can I fix Sunday dinner, Ma?"

Mrs. Williams nodded. "Of course, you can."

As they all sat around the table eating supper, Emma pointed out the things she'd done to help make the meal. "I made some of the pie crusts, and I helped cut up the meat to make bite sized chunks. Henri even taught me to touch meat! And I peeled potatoes, and made rice, and bread. I can cook, Ma!"

Mrs. Williams smiled at her daughter. "You've always been a good cook."

Henri didn't say anything as Emma excitedly explained everything else, she learned that day.

When the cake was put onto the table, Emma said, "I made that too. And I know how to make a simple frosting now too."

There were compliments all through the meal. Mr. Williams lavished praises on his daughter, and Henri could tell he was thrilled she was really learning to cook and not making up what to do along the way."

Henri smiled at Mrs. Williams. "Did your ma teach you to cook?" she asked.

"My ma died when I was three. I taught myself to cook, as I was the oldest of three daughters at that point."

"I'm so sorry for your loss," Henri said. Now Mrs. Williams's way of cooking made much more sense to her.

Mrs. Williams smiled. "I'm sorry for yours as well. I am glad you learned so much from her."

"I am too. I miss her every day. I can't even do a load of laundry without missing her."

As they were leaving, Emma excitedly hugged Henri goodbye. "Thank you so much! May I come back Monday and learn more?"

"I'd love that!"

"Can I bring my sisters?"

"Of course. Bring whomever you want." Henri was excited to teach the girls everything she knew about cooking.

"Can they bring their mother?" Mrs. Williams asked.

"Oh, that would make me so happy. Do you want lessons with your daughters or on your own?" Henri asked.

"We'll all do them together."

"Sounds good to me. If you're coming early Monday, bring more eggs."

Mr. Williams frowned. "What am I supposed to eat then?"

Henri laughed softly. "Why don't you come as well. We'll have eggs and bacon and toast."

"That sounds like the most delicious thing in the world," Mr. Williams said. "And my wife will learn to cook!"

As they left, Henri smiled at Roy. All the dishes were done up, and she was ready for bed. "I'm glad that went so well," she told Roy.

"I am too. I'm glad Ma is willing to have you teach her. None of her children knew the difference but Pa did, and he wanted better. Isn't it strange what will cause problems in a marriage? He'd put up with her cooking for twenty-five years."

She looked at her husband and asked a question that even surprised her. "How old are you?" How could she not know Roy's age?

"Twenty-three," he said.

"I thought you were about twenty-one!"

He shook his head. "I can't believe you didn't know that about me."

"Our relationship happened so quickly, I'm sure there are a great deal of things we don't know about one another." She paused, looking at him. "Do you know how old I am?"

"Old enough to be married," he said with a grin.

Henri laughed. "I'm eighteen, so yes, I'm old enough to be married."

"Glad to hear it!" he drew her into his arms. "Thanks for putting up with my worry about my ma's feelings."

"I'm sure I would have felt the exact same way in your shoes. It's hard when you want to help someone, and you just don't know how."

"I can understand that. But it all seems to have worked itself out. And I'm shocked that even with guidance, Emma could make a decent meal. She was worse than Ma!"

Henri shook her head. "She's not anymore."

*****

When Henri woke the following morning, she was surprised to see that Roy was already out of bed. He was never awake before she was.

She sat up and looked around the cabin, but there was still no sign of him. Where would he go this early in the morning?

She got up and dressed in her Sunday best, deciding there was no point worrying, and she started breakfast.

She hummed while she cooked, the same as her mother had always done. It was still hard for Henri to believe she'd gotten married without her mother at her side. The two of them had been so close. And then she was just gone.

It was a bit after sunup when she finished breakfast, and shortly after, Roy hurried into the cabin. "I got one!"

"I'm happy for you. One what?"

"A turkey! So, when you teach everyone to cook tomorrow, you can teach them to cook turkey and all the things that go with it."

Henri grinned. "Make sure your pa knows he's coming to supper tomorrow. And I'll invite my family. I hope it's a huge turkey!"

Roy shrugged. "Biggest turkey I've ever seen, but I don't know what you consider big."

She peeked out the door and saw he'd already chopped the head off the turkey. "Would it be rude if I taught your sisters to pluck the feathers, so I don't have to?"

"Not at all!"

*****

The next day was busy as they made all their favorites to go with the turkey. Everyone played a part in making the meal, and Henri made sure it was Mrs. Williams who made the bread.

By end of the long day, everyone was content and fed. Jared sat beside Emma after the dishes were done, and he said loudly, "You have become an amazing cook!"

"Only with the things I know how to cook," she said. "Henri has taught me a lot, but it's going to take me a long time to get as good as she is."

He grinned at her, and Henri turned to Roy. "What did you think of our turkey feast?"

"It was absolutely delicious." He dropped his voice. "Are you sure my ma made that bread?"

Henri laughed, nodding emphatically. "Tomorrow, we'll all learn to churn butter. My arms already ache in anticipation."

"Is the churn to your liking then?" he asked.

"I love it. It's absolutely perfect."

"Just like my beautiful wife."

After everyone had gone for the night, Roy took Henri's hand and led her to sit down on the side of the bed with him. "I'm sorry I was difficult about the cooking. So very sorry. You did a good thing teaching my family to cook, and I'm so happy you're the girl I married. I love you, Henri."

She turned and wrapped her arms around him. "I love you, Roy. You make me smile every day. My ma approved of you as a husband for me. She knew I had feelings for you from the time we left Missouri. She told me you were the man for me."

"I wish I'd had a chance to get to know her."

"I wish you had too." Raising her lips for his kiss, Henri knew that for the rest of their lives, she would live happily ever after with this man in their home. She was where she needed to be, and she couldn't wait to hold babies, though she was enjoying trying to make them as well, much to her surprise.

She thought it might be time to start knitting some baby booties, but she was a horrible knitter. Perhaps she could ask her mother-in-law to teach her how.

Epilogue

By the end of the next summer, Henri was working on her garden almost every day. Harvesting what could be harvested and weeding everything else.

It was late September, and she was in the garden harvesting her potatoes, when her pains came. Emma was beside her, helping her with the garden. "Are you all right?" she asked.

"The baby's coming!"

Emma smiled. "I'll go get Mrs. Mitchell. And Ma."

"Thank you!" Henri said.

She walked into the house and started boiling water, removing the sheets from the bed, and covering it in oil cloth. It wasn't the most comfortable thing in the world, but it would work.

Roy slammed the door open minutes later. She looked at him, "I guess you heard?"

"You didn't send someone for me? Of course, I'm going to be here for the birth of our child!"

"No, you won't. You don't need to be part of this. Go and work with the cattle. Your ma, Mrs. Mitchell, and I will do just fine on our own."

"But..."

"Go."

*****

It was almost twenty hours later when he was invited into the house to see his wife sitting up in bed, holding a baby wrapped in swaddling clothes. He walked to her and carefully sat on the bed, not wanting to hurt her. "Well?" he asked.

She smiled. "It's a little girl. I want to give her my ma's first name, and then your ma's first name for a middle name. Is that all right?"

"Absolutely." Roy thought for a moment. "So, she will be Nellie Norma Williams. Does that sound right to you?" he asked.

"It's perfect." She smiled up at him, and her face simply shone. "We made a beautiful baby."

"We did." He still hadn't had a chance to see the baby, but he knew it would be beautiful. "Good work, Mama."

"Good work, Papa," she said. "I love you, Roy."

"I love you more than I ever imagined I could love anyone."